The History of Voice Pedagogy

This ambitious publication draws from the knowledge and expertise of leading international figures in voice training in order to examine the history of the voice from an interdisciplinary perspective.

The book explores the historical arc of various voice training disciplines and highlights significant people and events within the field. It is written by voice specialists from a variety of backgrounds, including singing, actor training, public speaking, and voice science. These contributors explore how voice pedagogy came to be, how it has organized itself as a profession, how it has dealt with challenges, and how it can develop still.

Covering a variety of voice training disciplines, this book will be of interest to those studying voice and speech, as well as researchers from the fields of rhetoric, music, and performance.

This book was originally published as a special issue of the *Voice and Speech Review* journal.

Rockford Sansom, PhD, is a voice coach in theatre and a voice trainer in business and politics. He is the Editor of the *Voice and Speech Review* and an Assistant Professor of *Voice* at Louisiana State University.

The History of Voice Pedagogy

Multidisciplinary Reflections on Training

Edited by
Rockford Sansom

Routledge
Taylor & Francis Group

LONDON AND NEW YORK

First published 2019
by Routledge
2 Park Square, Milton Park, Abingdon, Oxon, OX14 4RN

and by Routledge
605 Third Avenue, New York, NY 10017

First issued in paperback 2020

Routledge is an imprint of the Taylor & Francis Group, an informa business

British Library Cataloguing-in-Publication Data
A catalogue record for this book is available from the British Library

ISBN 13: 978-0-367-72735-2 (pbk)
ISBN 13: 978-0-367-33460-4 (hbk)

Typeset in Minion Pro
by codeMantra

Publisher's Note
The publisher accepts responsibility for any inconsistencies that may have arisen during the conversion of this book from journal articles to book chapters, namely the inclusion of journal terminology.

Disclaimer
Every effort has been made to contact copyright holders for their permission to reprint material in this book. The publishers would be grateful to hear from any copyright holder who is not here acknowledged and will undertake to rectify any errors or omissions in future editions of this book.

Contents

Citation Information

The chapters in this book were originally published in the journal *Voice and Speech Review*, volume 13, issue 1 (March 2019). When citing this material, please use the original page numbering for each article, as follows:

Introduction

Chapter 1

Chapter 2

Chapter 3

Chapter 4

Chapter 5

Chapter 6
Singing Vocal Pedagogy in the Nineteenth Century Neapolitan School: The Work of Francesco Florimo
Giovanna Carugno and Cristina Patturelli
Voice and Speech Review, volume 13, issue 1 (March 2019) pp. 83–96

Chapter 7
The History of the Voice and Speech Trainers Association (VASTA)
Adrianne Moore
Voice and Speech Review, volume 13, issue 1 (March 2019) pp. 97–105

Chapter 8
The Rationale and History of Vocology
Ingo R. Titze
Voice and Speech Review, volume 13, issue 1 (March 2019) pp. 106–111

For any permission-related enquiries please visit:
http://www.tandfonline.com/page/help/permissions

Notes on Contributors

Erika Bailey is the Head of Voice and Speech for the American Repertory Theater (ART) at Harvard University, Cambridge, USA. At ART she has coached *Fingersmith*, *Night of the Iguana*, Eve Ensler's *In the Body of the World*, and Mark Rylance's *Nice Fish*. She is an Associate Teacher of Fitzmaurice Voicework®. She is also an Associate Editor of the *Voice and Speech Review*.

Giovanna Carugno has been a Lecturer in Arts Therapies at Roma Tre University, Italy; an Adjunct Professor of Performing Arts Studies at the University of Parma, Italy; and an Adjunct Professor of Music Education at the Conservatory of Salerno, Italy.

Lyn Darnley, PhD, performed in theatre, television, and radio before her career in teaching. She is the former Head of Voice, Text, and Artist Development at the Royal Shakespeare Company and the former Head of Voice at Rose Bruford College. In 2008 she was awarded the Conference of Drama Schools medal for Services to Actor Training. Since retiring, she has continued to work with actors, teachers, and university groups around the world.

Matthew Hoch, DMA, is an Associate Professor of Voice and Coordinator of Vocal Performance at Auburn University, USA. Hoch is the 2016 winner of the Van L. Lawrence Fellowship, awarded jointly by the Voice Foundation and National Association of Teachers of Singing. He actively performs art song, opera, chamber music, and in professional choral settings. He was recently appointed to the editorial board of the *Voice and Speech Review* and was a presenter at the 2017 Voice and Speech Trainers Association (VASTA) conference in Singapore.

Adrianne Moore is the Department Head and a Professor of Theatre Arts at Utah State University, Logan, USA, where she teaches voice and directing. She is also a freelance director and voice/dialect coach. She is the artistic producer and the resident voice/dialect coach for the Lyric Repertory Company. She is a member of Voice and Speech Trainers Association (VASTA) and a certified Associate Teacher of Knight-Thompson Speechwork.

Elizabeth Nash, PhD, was awarded a two-year Fulbright Grant to study opera in Germany and was a leading coloratura soprano in European opera houses for a decade. Since 1975, she has been the Head of Voice Studies in the Department of Theatre Arts and Dance at the University of Minnesota, Minneapolis, USA.

Cristina Patturelli collaborates with speech pathologist Massimo Borghese, whilst also working as a freelancer consultant, vocal trainer, rehabilitator, and opera singer. She is also a temporary teacher of music at a secondary school and singing teacher at a musical high school.

Carl Du Pont, DMA, has presented original research at conferences in Stockholm, Vancouver, and Indianapolis. He was recognized as one of Diverse Magazine's 2018 Emerging Scholars. He currently serves as an Assistant Professor of Voice and Coordinator of the Vocal Division at the University of North Carolina at Charlotte, USA. His scholarly focus is transformative inclusion in higher music education.

Rockford Sansom, PhD, is a voice coach in theater and a voice trainer in business and politics. He is the Editor of the *Voice and Speech Review* and an Assistant Professor of *Voice* at Louisiana State University, Baton Rouge, USA.

Ingo R. Titze, PhD, is a vocologist with formal training in physics, engineering, speech, and vocal music. He directs the National Center for Voice and Speech at the University of Utah, Salt Lake City, USA, and is a Distinguished Professor of Speech and Music at the University of Iowa, USA. He served as the first elected President of the Pan-American Vocology Association.

The Emergence of a Profession: The History of Voice Pedagogy

Rockford Sansom

The history of voice pedagogy is the rise of professionalism within the field, a chronological yet complex march from its origins as a subject of study to a cohesive profession. Voice (or vocal) pedagogy encompasses many kinds of teaching and training, so the starting point for voice pedagogy varies considerably depending on the specialization. Both western singing and public speaking training have origins dating to the ancient Greeks, but voice and speech training for the actor arguably begins in the nineteenth century. All the subjects intersect at times and have varying levels of organization throughout the centuries, but formalized vocal pedagogy as both a field of study and as a profession is nevertheless a relatively modern concept.

In her seminal examination on the history of professionalism, Larson [1977] 2017 argues that professionalized occupations require rigorous and often codified training that includes knowledge about the history of the profession, the skills required, and a code of ethics. Larson maintains that the original western professions (medicine, law, and the priesthood) still serve as a make-shift template for contemporary concepts of professionalism even though the definition and scope of professional occupations have grown exponentially in the past half century. In that, Larson believes that professionalism not only requires skill-based training in a subject, but also a knowledge of the scope and history of the field.

The articles in this issue seek to rise to that challenge. The authors give both the historical arc of voice training disciplines and detailed historical accounts within them. These articles offer a chronological account of how voice pedagogy came to be, how it has organized itself as a profession, how it has grown and dealt with challenges, and how it can develop. The *Voice and Speech Review* is an interdisciplinary journal, so fittingly this issue explores voice pedagogy history with an interdisciplinary lens. In recruiting and evaluating articles, I sought authors from various voice specialties such as singing, actor training, public speaking, and voice science, and I sought authors with unique historical perspectives.

I have organized the articles as chronologically as possible. The first three articles offer historical overviews of three major disciplines within voice training: voice for the actor, singing, and public speaking. While voice trainers do not all fall neatly into three categories, the breadth of these three articles offer a wide perspective on different kinds of voice pedagogy and how they evolved. Lyn Darnley begins the issue with "Theatre-Voice Pedagogy within the Royal Shakespeare Company: A Historical Perspective." As the former head of the Royal Shakespeare Company (RSC), Darnley explores the voice pedagogy history of the institution and its impact on actor training. She argues that many of the key creators and voice trainers at the RSC were pivotal figures in developing the modern concept of voice training for actors in the United Kingdom and in the United States. While the article centers on one prominent organization, in many ways it outlines essential concepts and chronicles the genesis of voice and speech training for theatre.

In "A Historical View of the Pedagogy of Public Speaking," Erika Bailey gives a historical account of how public speaking has been taught. As Bailey explains, the term "public speaking" arose in the eighteenth century, but Bailey goes deeper and explores the rhetorical and oratory roots of the field starting with the ancient Greeks and traces the development of public speaking through the centuries. The article also discusses current trends and how contemporary public speaking can interact with civic engagement. Matthew Hoch's "Historical Landmarks in Singing Voice Pedagogy" offers a similarly comprehensive view of singing pedagogy history. Arguably, more has been written on singing pedagogy than on any other kind of voice training specialty. Hoch accomplishes a Herculean task in synthesizing the wide body of western singing teaching literature that exists and creating a cohesive and practical narrative for the field. His article also explores the twentieth century rise of fact-based (or evidence-based) voice training, a consequential and notable trend throughout all of voice pedagogy.

The next three articles look at figures who deserve greater attention within voice pedagogy. Carl Du Pont in "Make the Door Open: Groundbreaking African American Teachers of Singing" reflects on significant African American teachers in the mid-twentieth century who broke color barriers in higher education voice departments. Recounting their struggles and triumphs, Du Pont asks that these figures take their place in the pantheon of influential singing teachers, and he discusses how their legacies influence training today. Elizabeth Nash continues this theme and looks at two eminent African American singing teachers in greater detail. In "A Historian's Journey with Sylvia Olden Lee and Camilla Williams, African American Opera Pioneers," Nash offers first-hand accounts of Lee and Williams's professional lives and how their influence changed the field of opera and changed Nash.

Francesco Florimo is primarily remembered as one of the world's greatest music librarians. But in "Singing Vocal Pedagogy in the Nineteenth Century Neapolitan School: The Work of Francesco Florimo," Italian authors, Carugno and Patturelli, argue that Florimo's significant legacy to singing training has unfortunately been lost to time. They offer historical evidence and accounts, and they examine his bestselling book on singing, which (as they argue) predates many modern ideas of singing and pedagogy.

The final two articles of the issue specifically examine professionalization in voice pedagogy. In "The History of the Voice and Speech Trainers Association (VASTA)," Adrianne Moore narrates the story of the organization. She explores its origins, growth, and major initiatives throughout the decades. VASTA is the sponsoring organization of this journal, and the *Voice and Speech Review* is delighted to publish a historical account of the organization. The final article comes from renowned speech scientist Ingo R. Titze, who is one of the founders of the field of vocology. In "The Rationale and History of Vocology," Titze discusses the birth of vocology, its relationship to audiology, and vocology's place within voice pedagogy and the voice profession.

The issue ends with an in memoriam to Cicely Berry, who passed away in the fall of 2018. Berry was the voice director of the Royal Shakespeare Company (RSC), and she is unquestionably a founding figure within voice pedagogy for actor training. Written by Berry's RSC colleague and friend, David Carey, this in memoriam highlights Berry's life and legacy. The fact that this tribute is in the journal's special issue on the history of voice pedagogy is only fitting.

Even with the contemporary professionalization of voice training, the arts and voice pedagogy still remain an oral tradition to some degree. Voice teachers not only impart skills and concepts about voice itself, but teachers also impart pedagogy either explicitly or implicitly to their students. In my experience, many voice teachers often educate in a manner and style similar to their influential voice teachers (Sansom 2016). At least in part, most voice teachers carry on some kind of historical legacy in their voice training.[1] In many ways, having an oral tradition within voice pedagogy seems appropriate; performing arts training is about becoming a storyteller, so passing on training through story is suitable to a degree. Nevertheless, as a novice teacher, I became curious about the larger field; I wanted to contextualize what I was teaching and learning. How did my personal voice training (what I had been taught and what I was teaching) fit into the entire field? What is the history and the scope of voice pedagogy? How are key figures and key movements in the field influencing my teaching in ways I may not understand? These questions ultimately pushed me into voice research and a more formal study of pedagogy—a journey that I am still on and cherish. As a researcher, writer, and editor, I am drawn to the "big picture": What has gone before me in voice and voice pedagogy and what will remain after my time? These questions and the questions I asked as a young teacher inspired me to develop this special issue. While the journal has had many notable articles examining topics and figures in voice pedagogy history during the journal's nearly two decades, there has never been a focused examination of the topic.

I am particularly proud of this issue. The Latin etymology of "editor" is "one who puts forth."[2] For this special issue, I am especially honored to do just that. When searching for voice pedagogy history as a young voice teacher, I never found a central source. Any knowledge I have about voice pedagogy history comes from putting together pieces over a lifetime of learning. While this issue is in no way comprehensive for all of voice pedagogy history, my hope is that it can serve as a starting place for both novice and veteran voice trainers alike who wish to explore how history can impact teaching, professionalism, and the artistic practice.

I hope you enjoy the issue.

Notes

1. For the record, I am *not* saying that teaching lineages are negative per se. I teach in a manner collected from many of my former teachers, and I also bring myself to the classroom. Passing on the best of what you have been taught is only good and natural. Rather, I am arguing that as a field we should also look beyond our own training and our own immediate teachers. We should explore the full scope of voice pedagogy.
2. For the complete etymology of the word, see the *Oxford English Dictionary*.

Acknowledgments

I wish to thank all of my previous voice teachers who ignited in me a passion for the arts and for the study of voice. I particularly wish to thank my earliest voice professors, Marilyn Shugart and Dr. Steven Chicurel-Stein, who both encouraged me to become a voice teacher. I am proud to carry on your legacy.

References

Larson, Magali Sarfatti. (1977) 2017. *The Rise of Professionalism.* New York: Taylor and Francis.
Sansom, Rockford. 2016. "The Unspoken Voice and Speech Debate [Or] the Sacred Cow in the Conservatory." *Voice and Speech Review* 10 (3): 157–168. doi:10.1080/23268263.2016.1318814.

Rockford Sansom
CMT-London, Savannah, GA, USA
✉ rockfordsansom@cmt-london.co.uk ⓘ http://orcid.org/0000-0002-9574-1308

Theatre-Voice Pedagogy within the Royal Shakespeare Company: A Historical Perspective

Lyn Darnley

ABSTRACT

This article examines the theatre-voice pedagogy history of the Royal Shakespeare Company (RSC), one of Britain's most long-lasting and prominent performing arts institutions. The article traces the history of the organization and highlights its influence in creating and cultivating the field of voice training, noting key figures such as Peter Hall, John Barton, Iris Warren, Michael Saint-Denis, and Peter Brook and their impact not only to Company but also to voice training. Cicely Berry's work and legacy is also explored. The author then uses autoethnographic techniques to analyze her time as Head of Text, Voice, and Artist Development at the Company. The article concludes with reflections on how the voice and text department at the RSC has shaped the field of voice training and gives implications for the future.

Introduction

Theatre-voice is a relatively young profession and is still striving for recognition in many cultures.[1] Every production that provides voice coaching will differ in its approach depending on the text, the space, and the director's/producer's vision. As a result, defining a specific pedagogy for voice and text coaching and training (theatre-voice practitioners undertake both activities in different situations) is a challenge for any theatre company. The Royal Shakespeare Company (RSC)[2] is the company I know best, so I will reflect on its pedagogy based on my own time there (1992–2014). I will consider its history, both published and anecdotal, and my experience as a participant observer. While documentation about past directors and practitioners who have influenced the work exists, this article hopes to give and overview of the development of voice work within the Company and insight into the practice in recent years.[3]

A Developing RSC Pedagogy

The RSC originally began in 1875 as the Shakespeare Memorial Theatre (SMT). The company received its Royal Charter in 1925, and it was renamed the Royal Shakespeare Company in 1961. Training actors was always part of its mission. When looking at the history of the RSC, general actor training was an initial primary focus, and voice work evolved as part of that training. The changing pedagogy of voice within the RSC resulted from the different ideologies of its chairmen and directors. Other influences came from the systems and fashions of voice teaching in the British drama schools at the time and from European theatre training. The Company, with its focus on classical theatre, needed a pedagogy that combined voice training with text work in order to advance specific performance skills and support the production of classic texts. Therefore, it is not possible to separate the pedagogy of voice from the pedagogy of text training, particularly in the early years, because the voice work grew out of the wider training ambition. What follows is a discussion of the complex influences on the RSC voice pedagogy.

Early Years

In 1875, formal British drama training was in its infancy. Elocutionists were responsible for training many British actors in the eighteenth and nineteenth centuries, but in the late nineteenth century, there was a desire for a more structured and recognized system of training so that acting would be respected as a skilled profession. A number of music schools offered speech training, and in 1882, the short-lived Royal Dramatic College opened, with Charles Kean, Charles Dickens, and William Thackeray among the trustees. Sarah Thorne's Margate school, established in 1885, was more successful and offered formal classes and an apprenticeship system. Tree's Academy of Dramatic Art was established in 1904 and later became the Royal Academy of Dramatic Art (RADA) (Sanderson 1984, 40).

The early archive of the RSC is peppered with references to a school of acting, partly due to difficulty attracting good actors to Stratford-upon-Avon because of its distance from London (Lowndes 1877).[4]

The initial inspiration for a training program came from the Meiningen company.[5] SMT Chairman Charles Flower stated,

> I am sure a Company might be trained to work here as it has proved to have done in Germany, and that its performance of Shakespeare's plays would be an intellectual treat such as yet has never been experienced in England. (Beauman 1982, 16)

Flower invited Frank Benson (also an admirer of Meiningen and his training methods) to bring his company to Stratford. At that time, Elsie Fogerty (who went on start what is now the Royal Central School of Speech and Drama [Central] in 1906) was working with Frank Benson's actors in his Hampstead school. Later, they attended classes at Central.

Archie Flower, Charles's nephew, who was SMT Chairman from 1903 until 1944, pursued the dream of a school for actors, and in 1923, an endowment scheme (Endowment Scheme 1923) was started in order to achieve this. The ambition was for "[t]he establishment and maintenance of a school of acting, the delivery of lectures, the establishment of prizes for essays, and other means for the advancement of the Dramatic Art" (1). There is no evidence of this being achieved, but so serious was the commitment to training and to the development of a school, that the Royal Charter of 1925 included this requirement:

> To advance and improve the dramatic art in Our United Kingdom and throughout the world by developing, extending and refreshing the skills and experience of the Corporation's employees by the production and presentation of dramatic performances of all kinds and by teaching and training and other educational activities including the establishment and maintenance of a school of acting and by other means. (*Royal Charter of the Royal Shakespeare Company* 1925, 1)

On July 12, 1934, Elsie Fogerty wrote to Archie Flower with a "Suggested Scheme" (Fogerty 1934), which outlined how selected students would be given three-year contracts with the SMT. They would serve an "apprenticeship" which included playing small roles, understudying, touring, and being hired out. They would continue to attend classes at the Central School including advanced work in "Voice, Speech and Movement, Text Study, Costume and Craft, Physics and Lighting" (Fogerty 1934). While this plan was never implemented, Fogerty's conversation with Flower suggests an interest in collaborating with an established school either because of funding limitations or because Flower realized his long-held ambition for a school in Stratford was unlikely to be achieved.

At a time when developments in European drama training were influencing attitudes to training in the UK, little was changing at the RSC; however, Iden Payne (SMT Director from 1934–1943) had a reputation for training his actors. It was said of Payne:

> At the moment I feel he thinks he can teach actors to speak Shakespeare. If he or anyone else had the available time it might be possible, but there is no time [...] the young members of the profession will not be taught. (Beauman 1982, 142)

Payne appointed a voice teacher, Denne Gilkes, to work on singing and voice. Gilkes trained at the Royal Academy of Music as a performer and teacher in 1910. From 1936 until her death in 1972, she was a teacher of voice production and singing for the Company. The actors she taught included Laurence Olivier, Vanessa Redgrave, and Paul Scofield. Presumably she applied singing techniques to spoken voice (Denne Gilkes Memorial Fund 2018). While there is evidence of her voice work, there is no evidence that she worked on productions, so it can be presumed that there was a separation between voice and the rehearsal texts and that text was the prerogative of the director. She may, of course, have worked on verse as a means of addressing voice.

Particularly influential on actor training in London was the 1936 opening of the London Theatre Studio (LTS), based upon the teachings of Michel Saint-Denis. It was not until the 1960s that this work fully impacted on training within the Company when voice teachers who had taught at the LTS worked with the actors. The best indication of the style of the LTS voice approach can be seen in the writings of Saint-Denis himself. His system, inspired by Jacques Copeau, used the actor as the starting point, encouraged playfulness, and worked against affectation (Rudlin 2000, 68). The same year, Michael Chekhov established the Chekhov Theatre Studio at Dartington College, teaching Rudolf Steiner's spiritual and philosophical voice method.[6] Michael Chekhov also developed Stanislavisky's system of psycho-physical training, which was the "complete integration of psychology and physicality" (Merlin 2001, 4).

In a different way, William Poel and other Oxford and Cambridge academics and directors influenced acting styles, and RSC verse speaking was subsequently influenced by the number of who became directors. Barry Jackson (director from 1945 to 1948) developed the talents of many young actors, among them Laurence Olivier, Ralph Richardson, and Paul Scofield. His directors included some leading influential teachers: Michael MacOwen, who later became head of the London Academy of Music and Dramatic Art (LAMDA); Nugent Monck, who followed Poel's principles; and Peter Brook. Brook worked at Stratford as an assistant director in 1947. He complained about the quality of the acting and doubted the validity of Jackson's casting policy, which was apparently to hire promising actors and coach them. Brook said,

> The young actors were all in the RADA image, stiff, conventional, and boring, either genuinely upper class, or stilted working class. My Romeo, for instance, was born with a Cockney accent. Now he would have kept it; then he had to learn to talk like a gentleman, and so he could not speak from his heart. (Beauman 1982, 184)

Anthony Quayle (director from 1948 to 1956) attempted to forge training links with both the Bristol Old Vic Theatre School and RADA, but to no avail (Quayle 1990, 161–162). With his own practical RADA training, he understood the need to develop actors capable of meeting the demands of both classic and contemporary theatre. Additionally, his connections with the new and experimental forces of Saint-Denis, Glen Byam Shaw, and George Devine[7] meant that the Company was to have an ongoing relationship with these influential minds for many years. Quayle had acted at the Old Vic in numerous productions often alongside Devine and had first-hand experience of the work of the Old Vic Company. By including Byam Shaw as Co-Director in 1952, Quayle connected the Company with the ethos of the LTS and the Old Vic School, an ethos which Peter Hall built upon when he took over as Director. When Hall succeeded Byam Shaw in 1959, it was he who finally provided actors with a structured training model.

Peter Hall: Balancing Truth and Form

The problem of Stratford's provincial location and the SMT's difficulty in attracting actors continued. Peter Hall (inspired by Brecht's Berliner Ensemble) addressed this issue by bringing leading London teachers to Stratford and creating a cohesive program of training with workshops led by theatre practitioners and experienced actors. Hall appointed John Barton as associate director in 1960 and Michel Saint-Denis and Peter Brook as resident directors in 1962. Saint-Denis was also charged with running a training program in Stratford (the RSC Studio), so began a significant period of actor training within the company. Rather than connecting with a drama school, Hall made training an integral part of the Stratford ensemble. He set about making the RSC a "teaching and research institution in order to create a new type of actor, comfortable in both classical and contemporary drama" (Chambers 2004, 141). In spite of this progressive move, voice teachers were not part of the creative team or involved in the rehearsal process.

John Barton

In 1960, Hall persuaded John Barton to leave Cambridge to teach verse-speaking in Stratford and become an associate director. Hall wanted to address the radically different styles of speaking verse. Actors were either reproducing the operatic and rhetorical style reminiscent of Benson, or they were speaking naturalistically in an attempt to express an emotional truth. There was a varied approach from directors, with Glen Byam Shaw insisting on actors acknowledging the end of the line and Tony Richardson telling them to "Just make it *real*, like any other speech" (Beauman 1982, 268). Hall felt that "Shakespearean verse-speaking was *dying* of naturalism" (Beauman 1982, 270).

A more naturalistic style had been a necessary reaction to the dated delivery preferred by some actors and it was also inevitable considering the influence of Stanislavski, Michael Chekhov, and Saint-Denis on training, as they all worked to avoid a declamatory style. Hall and Barton, both Cambridge graduates, developed a way of speaking that was perceived by critics as an RSC style, influenced by the literary criticism of FR Leavis and the poetic structure of George Rylands who, through the Cambridge Marlowe Society, had influenced many directors and actors as students. Among these were Peter Hall, John Barton, Trevor Nunn, Ian McKellen, and Michael Redgrave (Cribb 1999).

Hall said that, in 1960, "there was still a gulf of suspicion between theatre people and academics. [...] I think both sides have learnt to appreciate the virtues of each other" (Addenbrooke 1974 , 158). Hall succeeded in bringing academic thinking and theatre experimentation together successfully, but his beliefs about verse were strongly influenced by his time at Cambridge:

> For Hall the theatrical approach to a play, and to verse, was similarly analytic, beginning always from the text and searching it for meaning, symbolism, structure, and ambiguity. To that analytic, textual approach was married the influence of Rylands, and his understanding of shape, form, and colour of verse. [...] "Perhaps our ideal was to speak like Rylands, and think like Leavis." (Beauman 1982, 268)

Barton spoke of the need for verse work in the 1960s. What he said then is equally applicable today:

> Good actors, experienced in modern theatre or television or film work, are often out of their depth when confronted with a Shakespeare text. It takes time to become easy and proficient with Elizabethan verse, and can rarely be picked up in the course of rehearsing one particular play. (Addenbrooke, 2004, 203)

Ultimately, Barton had a profound and lasting effect on the Company's verse-speaking. From the practical perspective of the actor, in order to achieve what the director requires, it is necessary to develop not just technique, but a flexible and responsive voice. Hall's appointment of Barton suggests that he did not consider verse speaking to be the responsibility of the voice teachers he employed, and the two disciplines remained distinct. There is also no indication that he believed it was a responsibility to be shared.

The introduction of more structured voice training was therefore significant at this time, as was Hall's employment of teachers who were not from the Central, Bruford, and RADA traditions.

Iris Warren

Although Denne Gilkes was still teaching, Hall introduced new voice and movement teachers to develop the company's skills. Iris Warren taught voluntary voice classes in the late 1950s and early 1960s. *The Stratford Herald* reported on August 5, 1960:

> If you pass by the theatre on a Saturday morning, you will probably hear strange sounds floating from one of the upper windows—the note of a piano followed by a deep chorus of: 'Hey... hey ... hey ...hey.' That is also Iris Warren at work. When Peter Hall announced that his policy as director of the Memorial Theatre would include an assault on speech, Iris Warren was the obvious choice as consultant to the company. For the first time, a whole company would get voice-production classes from a noted specialist. (5)

Before the Second World War, Warren had worked with Michel Saint-Denis at the London Theatre School, and this relationship likely resulted in her teaching at the SMT. She had worked with the Stratford Ontario Festival in June 1956, and British director Michael Langham "first recognized the advantage of having a resident voice coach to work with the company while in rehearsal" (Ganong 1962, 33).

Little is known about Warren's approach other than what has been passed down by those who were influenced by her at the LTS and LAMDA, most significantly through Kristin Linklater (Linklater). It is believed Warren had no formal training but evolved her own teaching style through her interest in the individual voice. Edgar Wreford[8] was a private student of Warren, and Wreford notated 10 lessons and the exercises undertaken. It appears from these that her curriculum was conventional for the time. Thus, it must be assumed that what separated Warren from her peers was the way she framed exercises imaginatively and her style of teaching.

Saint-Denis and the Studio

Hall's greatest achievement was to bring together a dynamic mix of talented personalities who were able to pool their diverse and seemingly contradictory approaches to create a uniquely inspired experiment. He charged Michel Saint-Denis in 1962 with running a training program in Stratford (the RSC Studio), thereby creating an appropriate alternative to a school. The international and innovative group reversed the Company's previously isolated and provincial reputation, and the ensemble quickly became known as somewhere actors could extend themselves and work with some of the finest theatre practitioners in Britain.

> Hall and his colleagues challenged the traditions of the previous era, replacing painted cloths with solid sets, pictorial fantasy with realism, and stilted verse-speaking with a conversational style that (paradoxically) observed the iambic pentameter to the letter. Most importantly, they sought contemporary relevance in Shakespeare and introduced a repertory consisting of both classical and new work. (Trowbridge 2003, 1)

In his Studio, Saint-Denis continued the work that he had brought to England from Europe, which revolutionized British theatre training: involving the imagination and the art of mask and improvisation. Unlike physically expressive European theatre, British theatre was perceived as being essentially concerned with the delivery of the text. Hall attempted to balance a structured approach to text with imaginative and physical work. Saint-Denis had a significant influence on Hall's company and on its future:

> [Saint-Denis] taught a method of creating theatre that was essentially new on this side of the Channel. Insisting upon long rehearsal periods, the autocratic Saint-Denis looked for truth and meaning in improvisation; he believed that reality on the stage depended upon the discovery of a collective style, and expected his actors to bring to the work everything in their experience of life. (Trowbridge 2003, 65)

In the 1963 pamphlet "Three Men Look Ahead" from *The Crucial Years*, Saint-Denis writes,

It also includes further training of the actors' technical abilities, and of their creative imagination. Of these, the training of the imagination is by far the more important and the more complicated. [...] It goes from all forms of improvisation silent and spoken, tragic and comic, where the actor must have enough courage and talent to invent everything by himself. (Saint-Denis 1963, 23–25)

In a memo on September 10, 1962, Saint-Denis clarifies his firm commitment to ongoing voice classes:

We believe that there should be two sides to the Studio work: permanent basic training on voice and movement, verse-speaking and some kind of improvisation. This basic work should be permanent. That is that it should take place during the whole of the Stratford season and be suspended only during the most hectic periods of work from February to April. (Saint-Denis 1962, 1)

The Studio was for the use of all actors on a non-compulsory basis, except for specific Company calls. The program included mask, acrobatic, acting verse, voice, singing, movement, fencing, sword fighting, prosody, and poetics (Chambers 2004, 146). Tutors wrote reports on the work and on each participating actor. Geraldine Alford, who taught voice tutorials and who had also taught at the LTS, wrote that although she had full co-operation from those who attended, some benefitted more than others. She said of the standard:

Generally, I have been struck by the lack of any sound basic training or understanding of the use of the voice, so that bad habits are early set up—(which could easily be removed)—that are due to wrong training (or no training) and therefore ignorance and misconceptions about such basic things as breathing, tone, articulation, etc. become more deeply ingrained as time goes on. (Alford 1963, 2)

These comments suggest that the voice approach of the LTS, while considered different in style, addressed the same principles as more conventional teachers of the time. Actor Clifford Rose reported on verse-speaking classes:

I found generally a great interest and keenness, and a genuine desire for guidance—I think there is a very real need for "terms of reference" in this matter of speaking the verse both rhythmically and meaningfully—there seems to be much confusion about the way one should go about using the means at one's disposal and also what the "end product" should be like. (Rose 1963, 8)

Colin Chambers (2004) notes that while the Studio was carefully planned, the reality was that the demands of the rehearsal and performance schedules created obstacles to the implementation of the work. These problems were not confined to The Studio, and in later years the problem of time and scheduling interrupted the training; the ideal was often compromised because of the schedule, unpredictable re-rehearsals, and lack of space.

"The practical problems of integrating the Studio into the company's working life became more, not less acute and, despite the rhetoric, it enjoyed only a low priority within the burgeoning RSC empire" (Chambers 2004, 150–151). The Studio was short-lived and ran from 1962 to 1966 due to Saint-Denis's ill health and the Company's financial restraints. Nevertheless, its cultural legacy is substantial. His work influenced voice training through the greater use of imagination and improvisation in exercises. A clearer idea of his influence and approach to voice can be gleaned from his book *Training for the Theatre* (Saint-Denis 1982), although it is not known how much he influenced the voice teachers who worked with him or to what degree he was influenced by them.

Peter Brook

Brook's thoughts on classical text and verse speaking are expressed in his article "What About Real Life?" in which he speaks of the dilemma facing young actors when delivering Shakespeare:

> We must wean the actor away from a false belief: that there is a heightened playing for the classics, a more real playing for the works of today. The problem for the actor is to find a way of dealing with verse: if he approaches it too emotionally, he can end up in empty bombast; if he approaches it too intellectually, he can lose the ever-present humanity; if he is too literal, he gains the commonplace and loses the true meaning. (Brook 1963, 20–21)

Brook's awareness of the need to assist actors in the struggle to find a way to balance the commonplace with the scale of human emotion and heightened language in Shakespeare's texts continued to fuel training within the Company. Brook was later to become the major influence on Cicely Berry's voice and text work.

Hall's Legacy

The ensemble ideal and policy of continuing development for artists was initiated by Hall and continued in different ways by his successors. Hall was responsible for bringing to the newly named RSC a potent mix of personalities and approaches and for creating an ensemble that brought a dynamic combination of the European approach, experimentation, and academic thinking which filtered into British theatre through the actors, directors, and voice coaches who experienced it. Many of them went on to teach in drama schools. He was also the first RSC director to offer a comprehensive training program in acting, voice, verse, and movement, and he was the first to strive for a united approach to verse-speaking. Hall's influence on verse-speaking was considerable and divided actors and directors, some of whom felt he was over-rigid, but Hall stood by his ideals and insisted that actors in his productions spoke the text according to his principles.

Shakespearean academic James Shapiro observed Hall work in New York. Shapiro's article "Theater; Nurturing an English Flame in America" reports Hall saying,

> You will, please, all speak this the same way. And if you don't like it, don't be in it. It's not my method, it's the method and it works. [...] Shakespeare tells you when to go fast, when to go slow. You can read it like a score. He doesn't tell you the "why." "Why" is *your* problem. (*New York Times*, April 1 2001, 18)

Hall believed that the language and rhythms enhance the emotional life of the text if due attention is paid to the text, but he also supported the actor's right to make decisions about a character's motivation. Hall was aware of the need to keep questioning and reviewing the work, and in order to prevent the Company's practice from becoming entrenched, he said, "My successor had to belong to the next generation. It had to be someone who would challenge what I and my colleagues had done" (Beauman 1982, 292–293).

Trevor Nunn and Terry Hands

Hall was also responsible for bringing two young directors to the RSC: Trevor Nunn in 1964 and Terry Hands in 1966. Both would later become Artistic Directors. Nunn acknowledged the value of cross-generational knowledge sharing:

> John Barton proposed to me that he and I should collaborate on a re-working of Henry V, which had been part of the famous Stratford history cycle the previous year [...] I learned more about unlocking a Shakespeare text than any scholarship could have taught me. (as quoted in Barton 1984, ii)

Of the many positive aspects of Nunn's leadership, most significant was his establishment of The Other Place in 1973, where he introduced an era of experimentation that fueled training opportunities in the company. Nunn instilled a work ethic reminiscent of the laboratory ideals of Hall's Studio, but with his personal imprint:

> The emphasis was to be on self-improvement: the actors were asked to come in early, in tracksuits, for exercise sessions. The old company learning ideals were re-emphasized, and the notice boards bristled with rosters for classes—singing classes, movement classes, sonnet classes. It was to be, literally, a clean sheet, a fresh start. (Beauman 1982, 298)

Nunn believed in keeping the Company working as an ensemble. He blamed financial restrictions for getting in the way of an ideal ensemble ethic. "A mixed economy has meant that the RSC has never got beyond the appearance of 'ensemble' working" (Addenbrooke 1974, 183). He echoed Saint-Denis in his desire for permanence, ensemble, and training, and although his move to shorten actors' contracts seems to contradict this, he stated that "[t]he necessary work can only be done by permanence" (Addenbroke 1974, 183).

From a voice perspective, his most significant move was to appoint the voice teacher Cicely Berry in 1970. It was a combination of her imaginative approach and the creative and experimental energy of the RSC at the time which sparked new developments in voice and text and a more dynamic role for theatre-voice practitioners. Colin Chambers (2004) noted changes in verse-speaking under Nunn: "a more romantic speaking style and a sharper, more intensive use of colour" (61). How much influence Berry had on this "lighter touch" can only be speculated, but her role was far greater than that of her predecessors since she was a permanent member of staff and had access to the rehearsal room.

Terry Hands joined the RSC in 1966 to direct the touring Theatregoround. In 1978, he became Joint Chief Executive with Nunn, and in 1986, Hands took over the artistic leadership of the RSC. His contribution to training was largely through the informal opportunities created by the TheatregoroundFestival and the way in which he developed young actors of merit by giving them principal roles.

Cicely Berry

Cicely Berry's contribution to voice and text training in general is widely acknowledged. Her work is well documented, and she has written extensively about her approach (Carey 2003). So, I will consider her work in the light of her contribution to voice and text pedagogy in the Company and focus on how her work developed through her connection with actors and directors. Her text training for actors and directors is equal to John Barton's training and merits equal consideration.

Berry pioneered the role of the theatre-voice practitioner, which I am defining as someone who works specifically with performance-related vocal and textual needs of actors and directors.[9] She did much to promote the RSC as a theatre that develops the language skills of its artists. Through the establishment of a voice department, she provided a structured and consistent offer of artist training under Nunn, Hands, and Noble. It is with Berry that the voice work at the RSC moves from a pedagogy influenced by Saint-Denis to one more influenced by Peter Brook and Berry's own developing methodology.

Her training was at the Central School of Speech and Drama in the years when Gwynneth Thurburn was the principal. Berry, who describes her as "a most progressive and radical figure" (Berry (1987) 1992, 287), credits her with both inspiration and a sound, traditional training in voice, verse, and language. It is worth noting that Thurburn was trained by Fogerty who had worked with SMT director Frank Benson's actors and had trained at the Paris Conservatoire:

> What was important for me then was the time taken on the groundwork; groundwork in terms of metre, verse form, figures of speech etc., which opened the ear to the possibilities of formal language, and gave one the confidence to listen—and also to appreciate what was formal and what broke rules—in other words what was "other," and therefore interesting in another way. (Berry (1987) 1992, 287)

This groundwork would equip her well for working with heavily intellectual directors with defined ideas about verse speaking.

A very different influence on Berry was her husband Harry Moore, an American actor who died in 1978. He had trained in, and taught, the Method.[10] Through him she learned of actors' need to marry heightened text with naturalism.

> [But] two things had a great bearing on the work I did: one was an interest in language and how it could be communicated, and the other was the effect of Method work on the approach to acting and how that was interpreted here: I wanted to find out how these could interrelate. (Berry (1987) 1992, 288)

She realized that the Method would profoundly influence actor training in Britain but felt that there was a need to help actors trained in this way to communicate detail, character, and perceived "truth" to large audiences by focusing on the language rather than on volume and emotion. Playing heightened text with intimacy and detail in a large space is a challenge to young actors, who often find clarity and detail difficult to sustain while playing their objectives and conveying emotion (Berry (1987) 1992, 288). Finding synergy between old and new traditions became crucial, particularly when working on classic text.

Berry was not the first voice teacher at the RSC, but she was the first to be fully integrated into the rehearsal process. This allowed her to apply her work directly to the actor, director, and production. Developing the language role of the theatre-voice practitioner became Berry's passion. She was adamant that members of the voice department were acknowledged as working with both voice and text. The title of the Department was changed under Michael Boyd who understood that the skills of voice and language needed to be integrated.

Berry arrived at the RSC to work with an all-male group of directors. Nunn felt that the Company would benefit from a voice teacher used to training actors, but her work was concerned with more than clarity and well-produced vowel sounds. Berry was able to help and empower actors in a different way from the directors. Her approach to language differed from that of directors influenced by university-educated Poel, Rylands, and Leavis. She has acknowledged that she learned much from RSC directors, especially Barton, but her major influence was Peter Brook, a graduate of Oxford University committed to a non-intellectual starting point:

> It is always a mistake for actors to begin their work with intellectual discussion, as the rational mind is not nearly as potent an instrument of discovery as the more secret faculties of intuition. (Hodge 2000, 179)

Berry, like Brook, was keen to break the mold. She had a self-confessed enjoyment of anarchy.

Evolving a Theatre-Based Approach

Berry's text approach evolved in rehearsal rooms where she sought practical ways for actors to access the text without losing the integrity demanded by contemporary training or destroying the director's process. Her work is evidence of what can be generated in a creative environment. Trevor Nunn wrote in the foreword to *The Actor and The Text*, "[She has] an explorer'sobsession, a radical's fervor and a philosopher's generosity; she is a voice teacher with a mission. Her uniqueness and authenticity have made her work a fundamental part of the RSC's achievement" (Berry (1987) 1992, iv). Berry recalled her early years at the RSC in an interview with *Plays and Players*:

> When Trevor Nunn took over, he thought there should be a voice director attached to the company. "He went to somebody else first," she laughed, "and then came to me. I didn't know anyone with the RSC but I had taught a number of well-known actors like Sean Connery and Peter Finch at my private studio in the West End." (Parker 1985, 32)

Initially, Berry worked four days a week pioneering her work:

> To begin with, I only worked with people who knew of me, like Judi Dench, who had worked with me at the Central School of Drama. But some actors, quite nicely, didn't want to know about it, which was fair enough. But there were these young ones like Roger Rees and Ben Kingsley and, as they came up, the whole thing gradually grew. (Parker 1985, 45)

She spoke of how she worked to win the trust of directors who, at first, were nervous about her intervention.

> Luckily, now nothing is questioned but when I first came it was quite a different matter. Directors were very suspicious. It took me seven or eight years before nobody questioned what I was going to do with them. Directors nurse their actors very carefully. You can do a lot of damage if you give insensitive criticism or stir it at all between the director and an actor. (Parker 1985, 46)

Although she valued her training highly, she was aware that some traditional voice exercises developed at Central School were not ideal for contemporary actors. The rigid breathing system, known as rib-reserve, was taught to everyone regardless of size and shape and created tension in many people, particularly women. While this system had been practiced by actors since the early part of the twentieth century, it began to meet with criticism and from the 1970s it was thought to restrict vocal spontaneity:

> I taught this way for a while and then I began to think it was over-disciplined and over-controlled. Particularly since I've been with the RSC, I've developed a way of working that means finding the breath and centering the body but not being quite so over-controlled. The old way made one think that the voice was too much like an instrument we use, rather than a part of ourselves. For instance, we have to develop our breathing so that it is to do with what we want to say, deeply rooted in our emotions. (Parker 1985, 55)

Inspiration from Peter Brook

Berry was inspired by Brook's ideas when in 1970 she worked with him on *A Midsummer Night's Dream*:

> He used detailed exploration of improvisatory techniques to dislodge actors from reductive psychological behaviourism, and, as they began to tap other energies, Brook was able to recognize their creative primacy. (Marshall and Williams 2000, 175)

Inspired by his ideals, Berry devised improvisational text exercises within strongly defined structures to, like Brook, dislodge actors from pre-conceived ideas and allow them to work freely and spontaneously with the voice and language. Brook's example allowed her to find routes into the actor's intelligence physically, rather than trying to understand the text academically. Brook and Berry were like-minded with regard to what is perceived as "good speech." Brook gave this advice to an actor in *A Midsummer Night's Dream*:

> All that you are doing, is getting the words out well. The moment you go into pathos, you are playing the wrong line completely. If you cultivate emotional states, you cannot find anything. When your emotions swamp your sense of what is happening second-by-second, you are wrong! It is the difference between generalized emotion and being with the intimate course of the unfolding words. In it every word is an action. (Selbourne 1982, 79)

The resulting spontaneity does not lead to a loss of vocal focus but rather sharpens it.

Berry shares Brook's commitment to "the ritual properties of language," but not his interest in the formulation of other languages because of his dissatisfaction with "the language of words" (Selbourne 1982, 77). Berry has remained constant in her belief that words, when physically embodied and used with muscularity and commitment, suffice, and that their soundscape is an intrinsic part of the multi-layered texture of meaning. In an RSC rehearsal room, the director usually begins with a detailed analysis of the text. The voice coach, meanwhile, provides the physical and organic exploration of the language, offering a balance to the cerebral work. Cicely Berry works with actors to release the *turmoil* and dynamic of the language and to explore the rhythmic changes and contrapuntal points within the iambic line. This is not to say that verbal anarchy is Berry's objective.

Brook, like Berry, believed that a solid skill-base must be acquired by actors; the voice, like the body, must be open and free. They shared a desire to *unsettle* the actor's habitual patterns; to develop dexterity in the individual and in the ensemble; and to encourage actors to articulate different impulses and exchange energies.

In the work of Brook, Berry found a strong commitment to the idea that "[t]o speak words should alter you" (Berry [1987] 1992, 289). "Words change people," she states frequently, but the change she refers to is empowering, political change, rather than therapeutic, personal growth (289). Her search is for a way for modern actors to access classical language and communicate it meaningfully to a modern audience. Her starting point is not the literal meaning of the words, but the non-cerebral, visceral, and physical power of vowels and consonants.

Brecht was a major influence on both Brook and Berry. Brecht, like both Berry and Brook, wished to avoid a received sound. Like Berry, he advocated integrating acting exercises with technical exercises in order to avoid formulaic acting. But Berry is the most direct link with the language aspects of Brook's RSC work, and she has maintained his early influence within the Company through her work on text and language.

Berry's Voice Pedagogy: Creating Chaos Out of Order

For actors who become locked in a "safe, well-behaved," and predictable pattern or become obsessed by the sound of the voice, the creation of a situation in which they can no longer hold the pattern often frees them to be spontaneous and able to "invent" and newly mint the language. The relief that young actors often feel when they are enabled to explore the "chaos within the form" is palpable. MaGuiken (2000) said "I thought it *had* to be *smooth*, that it was what we were aiming for" (3). This is a response typical of many young actors. Berry's exercises often make actors physically uncomfortable and "knocked off-center" by creating circumstances that do not allow them to over-control. This theme was not only evident through work with the acting company, but it was also clear in how her exercises evolved, while working with teachers and youth groups as part of the RSC Education Department:

> Over the years I have run countless workshops on Shakespeare in schools, in community groups, and also many weekend workshops for English and Drama teachers: this taught me a huge amount, and gave me a further perspective. (Berry (1987) 1992, 288)

Work with Schools

Interaction with large groups of young people, many of whom were initially resistant to the work, meant that she had to find ways of stimulating a desire and need to speak and a sense of the physicality of language. Actors, too, needed to be provoked to shed the restrictive *hold* that often results from a desire to be clear and correct. They had to give themselves permission to go with the rhythm or break out of it, rather than be regularly paced and over-respectful in their delivery. She asserted that some actors feel they must speak in a style and accent unrelated to their own, which results in a sound once removed from themselves. Berry encourages exploration of the sensation of shaping words rather than listening to the quality of voice. She focuses on sensation-led placement of consonants, spatial and emotional quality of vowels, physical vibration of the voice in the bony structures, and changes in the pulse of rhythms. By releasing the voice through the body and the words, the quintessential power of the language is released. She encourages a need to be heard so that audibility and clarity cease to be an issue.

Meaning and Clarity

In Berry's work, the voice, speech, and word are reconnected with the body and the breath impulse. This connection peels back layers of logic to find the essential energy and vibration in the muscle and sound of the words. Working in this way *reveals* the meaning, thereby reducing the need for intellectual analysis. While using Berry-influenced exercises with a group of young writers, one student reflected, "This is *physical* text analysis, you don't have to do any more" (personal communication, June 2000). Berry's work proves that intellectual analysis is not the only route to understanding complex text, but it is also borne out by actor feedback. Nicholas Jones, a leading actor, commented on February 18, "Cicely Berry knows where clarity lies." This was said by an actor working with her on the text of *A Midsummer Night's Dream*: "She knows this better than most directors" (Jones 2000, 1). Berry always works to provoke a spontaneous response in actors so that they are never able to declaim or emote. She has waged a battle for sense over sentiment. She demands that actors play situation, not emotion, and is committed to the need to make language uncomfortable. "Language," she often says, "should cost" (personal communication, March 2005). These are the passions which set her apart from her predecessors and many of her peers.

Speaking and Listening

In Cicely Berry's work, the importance of listening is paramount:

> It is all about listening, isn't it? Being able to listen to what is happening, not only the line or the modulation of the lines, but in the spaces between the words, and that is very important with modern writing. The spaces between the words take us into that imaginative world. (Berry 1998, 2)

Brenda Bruce described the detailed listening involved in working on verse with Cicely Berry and Terry Hands:

> Generalisation was not allowed; we had to be specific; we had to learn to look each other in the eye and *tell* the sonnets to each other. Cicely Berry took speeches at random; we sat in a circle and, starting with the first word, spoke one each, in correct sequence, slowly, halting at first; but gradually one forgot oneself, picked up the word and passed it on to the next actor. We learned to *listen* to the actor on the left and *give* to the actor on the right. With practice it became like a near-perfect relay race; accepting and passing, we became one voice. [...] difficult at first, but when carried into rehearsal most helpful. (Brockbank 1985, 94)

Berry describes language as inclusive in an attempt to convey the many levels on which language operates. Most of her exercises find ways to release, illustrate, and excavate the complexities of language. She does not give information, but rather allows actors to make the language their own and has brought to voice and text work a human, non-cerebral dimension that addresses the needs of actors.

Berry writes as she teaches. She had a strong influence on text teaching in many drama schools from the 1980s onwards. When asked how her methodology came about, Berry said, "I realized, in my forties, that I had a philosophy about the teaching of text that was not only innovative but empowering for the actor" (personal communication, March 2005). She has never lost sight of where the work must begin. She said,

> Actors come with ideas about feelings and emotions. But I don't think you can understand Shakespeare completely until you start to speak it aloud. You can understand it at many levels when you read it, but until you speak it, until you get round the muscularity of that language you don't totally understand it, it doesn't alter you. (personal communication, June 1998)

Undoubtedly, it is with Berry that there ceased to be a separation between voice and text within the Company. The close relationship between Berry and Barton and their shared values were instrumental in bringing the two disciplines together. Both of them, working on the same text, but differently, gave directors and actors insight into the myriad possibilities of the text and performance choices.[11]

Adrian Noble

Under Adrian Noble (from 1991 to 2003), the voice department grew. Noble supported and valued voice work and continued to hold occasional full-company training sessions with Berry and Barton when the busy schedule allowed.

The Other Place[12] offered voluntary development projects and workshops when possible (usually toward the end of the season when productions had opened) with classes in theatre skills including singing, movement, text workshops from the voice department, and acting with distinguished visiting directors such as Augusto Boal and Declan Donnellan. Under Noble the RSC Fringe festival thrived, offering members of the company opportunities to extend their skills in acting, writing, and directing and bringing together company members from all departments, including the administration. Occasional poetry programs were staged by Berry, offering younger actors the opportunity to develop their verse-speaking skills. The voice department supported productions in the Fringe, offered solo voice sessions, and offered workshops for the RSC Education Department and the Shakespeare Centre.

The Academy Company

In 2003, Michael Boyd succeeded Adrian Noble as Artistic Director. Noble's final training initiative was to establish an Academy company in the summer of 2002, giving intensive training to 16 newly graduated actors. This was very different from the loosely structured training offered at The Other Place since the newly graduated actors were not integrated into the main company but were part of a satellite training company:

> We are planning that the Academy will be very much like a theatrical apprenticeship, with a program of intensive study complemented by performance of a Shakespeare production at the Royal Shakespeare Theatre[13] [RST] as part of the Summer Festival Season. (Noble 2002)

Classes were held in the morning and rehearsals in the afternoon and evening, allowing postgraduate actors to delve deeply into formal language, voice, movement, and acting. The inference was that such an Academy would become permanent. The pilot program, with director Declan Donnellan, ran for 12 weeks, culminating in a production of *King Lear* which was eventually staged in the Swan not the RST. Actors were paid the Equity minimum. The Academy coincided with the hand over from Noble to Boyd. Many actors felt that the system operating at the time (which allowed all actors to learn informally through rehearsal, performance, voluntary classes, and projects at The Other Place) could not be improved upon by an academy catering to a small group of actors. While the young actors were given intensive training, they also lost an opportunity to learn by watching their more experienced colleagues. After consultation and review, Michael Boyd chose to address the requirements of the Royal Charter more closely than previous Artistic Directors.

The Artist Development Program

Boyd, after graduating from Edinburgh University, received a British Council fellowship with the Malaya Bronnaya Theatre in Moscow. Following a successful directing career, he became the Artistic Director of Glasgow's Tron Theatre from 1985 to 1989. He worked frequently at the RSC from 1994 and in 2001/2002 won the Olivier Award for Best Director for *Henry VI Parts 1, 2* and *3* and *Richard III*.

Boyd believed that actors should work and train together in order to build skills and a common practice, and he placed the need for continual development at the heart of his ensemble ethos, a bold move in a theatre culture that does not traditionally embrace a notion of ongoing development of actors within an ensemble company. After a formal review of the Academy in May 2003, Boyd chose not to pursue a satellite training company, but to fully integrate training inside the ensemble. A press release published on Boyd's appointment, stated,

> The Ensemble acting company will rehearse, train and perform together over a period that is twice the rehearsal time that is usual in the UK. Creating and nurturing the Ensemble will inject a spirit of experimentation and enquiry into the fabric of the company. Longer rehearsal periods create a freedom for directors and actors to test ideas and take risks, providing the opportunity to develop the best possible performances. Actors from this year's Ensemble will also form part of our acting company for 2005, so that over time, audiences can follow their work as they perform in many, varied roles for the RSC. (Royal Shakespeare Company 2002, 1)

Boyd began developing the Artist Development Program immediately and the first training sessions were scheduled for the *Tragedies* ensemble in December 2003.

Tragedy Season Training and Rehearsals 2003/2004

All actors were contracted to attend training which was conducted over an initial period of one full pre-rehearsal week, followed by daily pre-rehearsal warm-ups and one half-day of training in each of the subsequent nine rehearsal weeks. The final two weeks of rehearsal did not include training. To begin with, for financial reasons, the training was given only to the 36 members of the Royal Shakespeare Theatre ensemble.[14]

On December 8, 2003, Boyd welcomed the ensemble to a new and historic phase in the life of the RSC and spoke about "[h]ow we make the time that actors spend at the RSC a time when you really do grow" (Boyd 2003). Peter Hall, John Barton, and Cicely Berry were present, as well as the actors and the creative team. Boyd spoke to the ensemble about the training they would undertake. He mentioned the challenges the language presents for actors and of the "connected-ness" the plays have with the family, political structures and social conditions in our time, saying,

The heightened language of the classics and Shakespeare and the direct language of the contemporary world are separated at your peril. Character, narrative and metaphysical ideas need not be separated and contemporary work at its best should aspire to this. (Michael 2003, 1)

The program was delivered by RSC practitioners, current directors, directors with historical links with the Company, and professionals from outside the organization with specialist skills and knowledge. Those leading the work were Michael Boyd, Peter Hall (verse and text) John Barton (verse and text), Cicely Berry (voice, verse, and text), Ralph Williams (literary academic, University of Michigan), Peter Gill (director), Dominic Cooke (director), Jonathan Bate (Shakespeare academic), Alex De Silva (Capoeira artist),[15] Liz Ranken (movement director), Lyn Darnley (voice and text coach), Max Atkinson (rhetorician and academic), John Burgess (director), Rob Clare (text coach), Sue Laurie (Alexander technique teacher), and Richard Cave (Feldenkrais practitioner).

The voice, verse, text, rhetoric, and language content are evidence of Boyd's belief in the importance of vocal and verbal skills. It was clearly stated by both Boyd and Hall that verse must remain at the heart of the training. Their concern reinforces the belief of many voice coaches that, while a broad training is desirable for today's actors, the result has been a reduction in time dedicated to practical spoken work on poetry and dramatic verse.

Approaching the Verse

Hall, Barton, and Berry held a discussion on language and verse. Although all three approached the work from their own perspectives, they shared a mutual aim to focus on language and on building a performance starting from the words. What differed was the degree of formality. Hall was the most rigid with strong opinions about metre, pace, and avoiding breathing mid-line. Barton claimed originally that he had been more formal in his approach than Hall but had become more flexible, allowing actors more choice and freedom. Cicely Berry's approach was the most flexible, focusing on releasing language spontaneously. Essentially, all three advocated frequent practice in speaking classic texts.

After a class in the second week, actors were asked what useful clues and strategies they would take away. The responses were as follows:

- To note when the language changes from rational language to language rich in metaphor and imagery, and to consider why this change has occurred.
- To remember that Shakespeare's habit of mind was antithetical.
- To always find the need to speak and the desire to share the words.
- To drive the thought through to the end of a line and/or thought.
- To know that even when using pace, you can still allow words space.
- To trust the words to release the character.
- To be always present and specific and never generalized.
- To trust that the meaning reveals itself through the language.
- Never to make a judgement based on the first line of the verse, but to allow the gear changes to become apparent, allowing the full intended meaning to emerge.

The group discussed the Elizabethan actor's ability to read and interpret text quickly in a way similar to a musician reading music, and the sixteenth-century use of the word "character" (meaning a symbol for writing rather than the contemporary use meaning "personality").

Observation of the language sessions revealed considerable variation in the ease with which actors handled the language. Both age and experience contributed to this disparity. Actors who had worked regularly with the Company displayed a greater willingness to play, explore, and risk. This was possibly connected to familiarity with the process and the methods. The technical ability of actors varied, with some younger actors less able to phrase and interpret instantly than their more experienced colleagues, who displayed an impressive vocal and interpretative muscle built over years of practice.

Further work on verse was included in voice and movement sessions led and team-taught by Liz Ranken (movement and yoga) and Lyn Darnley (voice and text). Although the content differed, the work was similar in approach to the work of Cicely Berry. Contemporary poetry was used to generate rhythm and imagery, which was explored physically and vocally. An important function of the first period of the training was to build an ensemble ethos, create a common vocabulary for the verse and text work, and create vocal and physical flexibility and stamina.

Physical Skills

The voice and movement classes focused on establishing alignment, a low breathing pattern, releasing habitually held tension, and creating strength, stamina, and flexibility in body and voice. Vocal and physical rhythms and energies were explored and, when possible, applied to the speaking of text. There was also an emphasis upon maximizing physical and vocal communication, and imaginative expressiveness. Verse was used as a starting point for work on rhythm, breath, vowels and consonants, weight, effort, and energy. The Alexander and Feldenkrais classes had a positive impact on body and voice.

Ranken and I also worked with actors as part of the creative team and conducted solo classes building physical, vocal, and text skills linked to rehearsals. The usual stage fighting and military skills were undertaken regularly. Similarly, production-related dialect and text work was addressed in rehearsal calls. Singing was coached individually by John Woolf (Head of Music). Limited time prevented further group singing work, though more was requested by actors and was provided in all subsequent training programs.

Intellectual Work and Research

A variety of lectures focused on the language of the plays in rehearsal. Talks were entitled: "Shakespeare's Tragedies" (Ralph Williams), "The Tragedy Genre" (Jonathan Bate), and the "History of Tragedy" (John Burgess). There was also an afternoon on rhetoric led by Max Atkinson. Time was spent considering the different writing styles of early translations of the Bible (specifically extracts from the Tyndale text of 1525–1526 and the Coverdale Version of 1535) in order to understand more completely the development of Shakespearean language. Further typical production-specific research work and intellectual investigation of historical and sociological aspects of the plays was undertaken by actors during rehearsal.

Challenges

The 2003/2004 pilot program created a series of challenges for actors and coaches. For voice and movement practitioners, the objective was to extend the ensemble's disparate skills by doing technical work both in isolation and in response to the creative needs of the productions. It became evident that a particular challenge in a mixed-aged and multi-experienced ensemble was to meet the needs of the young, while offering some level of extension for senior actors. A small amount of opposition was detected early on in the program from a few actors. Time pressures with directors needing more rehearsals sometimes resulted in canceled sessions. As weeks went by, fatigue became a challenge for some mature actors. The feedback from actors was positive, however, and suggestions were taken into account for future planning. The core program always included the fundamental skills which focused on the performance of classical text: voice and verse speaking, rhetoric, movement, music, and the historical and social background of the plays. All other sessions were related to the specific demands of the production. In this way, the RSC voice and text pedagogy was maintained and then enriched by other disciplines.

The Artist Development Program in Subsequent Years

From the 2004/2005 season onwards, the design and co-ordination of the Artist Development Program became the responsibility of the voice department. Each program was created in response to the wishes of the directors and the nature of the productions. Mask work, *Commedia dell'Arte*, drumming, puppetry, a cappella singing, dream work, and other specialist skills, as well as research visits and lectures, were provided. The core training continued with verse, text, and rhetoric and with pre-rehearsal classes in voice and text, movement, and group singing. Training was extended to the Swan productions so that all actors in the RSC participated.

Early in the rehearsals all actors were given voice and movement sessions on the stage on which they would perform, in order to familiarize themselves with the space and acoustic. As many companies rehearsed in London, day-trips to Stratford-upon-Avon were taken. Boyd also introduced several other significant changes which influenced vocal skills:

- Voice and movement warm-ups were offered before every performance.
- He established a system whereby one dedicated voice coach worked on each production or themed season, allowing the voice coach to be acknowledged as a member of the creative team. Having one dedicated voice and text coach was popular with directors and fulfilling for coaches
- Cicely Berry and John Barton (who were both now working in a more advisory capacity) gave workshops to all companies in the early weeks of rehearsal.
- Voice placements were established in 2004 in order to expose newly trained voice coaches to the demands of professional theatre and to develop their skills in theatre-voice by participating in the training program, observing rehearsals, working with other coaches, and conducting warm-ups and eventually individual sessions. While assisting the voice coach on productions, they also undertook understudy coaching. There were opportunities for running workshops with the

RSC Education Department and involvement in outreach projects. A movement placement was established soon afterwards.

- Michael Boyd appointed Struan Leslie as Head of Movement in 2008, providing a full-time movement department to cater for the physical well-being of the Company as well as co-coordinating production-specific choreographers and movement directors. A greater emphasis on movement brought improved flexibility and alignment and subsequent vocal benefits.
- The culture of training and openness within the ensemble meant that voluntary sign-up sessions for ongoing solo classes were well attended.
- Boyd's inclusive approach meant that he encouraged the department to develop connections with drama schools and universities, thereby reaching promising young actors, writers, directors, and voice coaches interested in developing their text skills. Trainee directors and voice coaches as well as members of the Actors Centre, London, and amateur theatre companies were offered similar programs. Workshops were free of charge and included theatre tickets and on-stage sessions. Rather than the Company looking for support from drama schools, as it had done earlier in its history, it was able to reach out to a new generation of theatre practitioners and give them insight into a classical company.
- Under Boyd, the understudy run (directed by the assistant director) was given an additional performance, which was open to the public at a reduced price. These performances were well attended, and the quality of the understudy work improved enormously. The improvement in confidence and preparedness could be seen when understudies were called upon to step into a leading role. Younger actors with minor roles were given the opportunity to stretch themselves artistically and develop new skills.

Significantly, Boyd changed the name of the voice department to the "Voice, Text and Artist Development Department," thereby recognizing the full contribution made by voice coaches.

A Personal Perspective

When I joined the RSC in 1992, most British voice teachers had been trained in a similar way, based on the pedagogy of the Central School. Teachers often worked in more than one drama school, which tended to produce a uniformity of actor training, and teachers often came from a performance background themselves, where they too had been taught in the Central School/RADA/Bruford system. The only voice training course was Central School's world renowned specialized Advanced Diploma in Voice Studies which had started in 1982 and was run for the first four years by Helen Wynter. The course was small with between 10 and 12 students and attracted students from many countries. It had a strong practical bias and included vocal anatomy and physiology, phonetics, text, and Alexander Technique. Wynter was succeeded by David Carey, who had been Cicely Berry's assistant at the RSC.

Teacher training in the UK now differs considerably, with postgraduate courses in voice studies offered by Birmingham School of Acting, Guildford School of Acting, Guildhall School of Music and Drama, and Bristol Old Vic Theatre School. Access is wider, and training is broader with graduates going on to teach presentation skills, accent reduction, dialects, and singing. Intensive short courses in methods such as Linklater, Lessac, Estill, Fitzmaurice, and Nadine George are widely available; consequently, actors are now less likely to share a common approach and have much more diverse training experiences. It cannot be assumed that they have a common language, and it is important for the coach to be familiar with their preferred working method.

By 1992, Berry had taken a more consultative, though still active, role as Voice Director, and the Head of Voice was Andrew Wade. While a distinct vocal pedagogy was not stated, members of the team shared similar training with roots in the Central/ Bruford/RADA traditions and a common language and understanding. Goals and objectives were regularly considered, as were the individual demands of each production. Voice work was done alongside—and was indivisible from—text work, so that specific work on tone, intonation, inflection, rhythm, and metre had context and related to performance. Active encouragement was given for healthy voicing and a speech therapist came in to talk to actors about voice care. A pedagogy of text, meanwhile, was more clearly defined. Cicely Berry's approach underpinned the work. Once productions were in the repertoire, actors could sign up for ongoing individual work and group workshops. Voice warm-ups were offered three times a week and included physical and vocal work and poetry.

John Barton's verse work also had a strong influence on verse speaking. All rehearsals were supported by company and solo voice and text sessions from members of the voice department. Under Noble members of the voice department worked on all productions, sitting in on rehearsals and offering voice work to the actors and understudies. In order for this to be beneficial, it was important to develop a working relationship with the director, assistant director, and other members of the creative team since not all directors knew the benefits of having a voice coach on the team, or how to use their skills. It was a relationship that needed negotiation. Under Boyd, each production was allocated a specific voice practitioner who worked solely on the production, which allowed for a more creative and intense relationship with the production. Although I had spent 13 years teaching in a conservatory, I quickly learned that voice work in a theatre company differed considerably, and the skills of a theatre-voice practitioner could only be learned experientially. Experience in the undergraduate training conservatoires, while essential, does not fully equip a teacher for theatre-voice work and the differences demand a flexible pedagogy. These differences include the following:

- A company of actors usually has a wide range of age and experience.
- Most actors will have trained in a conservatoire whereas others may have studied the subject at a university or youth theatre, or they will have not trained at all.
- Some actors will have worked regularly on stage while others may have worked predominantly in film or television and have little stage experience. Older actors may have gained their early experience the weekly or monthly rep system.
- The relationship between a voice teacher and a student differs from that of an actor and a voice coach. Some actors have had difficult relationships with voice teachers, and the voice coach needs to negotiate and strive to turn negative history into positive engagement.

- Students are more likely to be open to the teaching style and methodology of the institution, whereas actors often come with a preferred voice practice. It is important to identify the actor's preferred style of working and not to contradict or undermine their methods.
- Voice and text work in the training setting are often separated in order to allow repetition and support vocal development, and while vocal exercises are essential, in the theatre setting they need to be appropriately directed toward each production or performance situation.
- The balance between teaching and coaching differs, with more weight being given to coaching in the theatre setting.
- Some training institutions follow a single methodology, but in a theatre where actors come from different training backgrounds, eclecticism is necessary. I found it important to familiarize myself with the methods of the major drama schools and to keep abreast of new approaches. I am not suggesting someone with certification in a specific method cannot work happily with actors trained in another system; many do so very successfully, but it is essential to put the actor's needs before a single methodology.

During the enormously rewarding 22 years I spent at the RSC, there was a culture of knowledge-sharing, providing opportunities to observe and learn from directors, colleagues, and visiting experts in their field. It was rewarding to see actors develop as a direct result of extended contracts, Boyd's understudy system, and the ensemble training ethos. Most rewarding was the change of the department title to voice and text as it acknowledged the team's creative role and brought together the two fundamental aspects of vocal communication in the theatre.

Michael Boyd was knighted for his services to theatre and left the RSC in 2013. Gregory Doran succeeded him as Artistic Director, and it was his decision not to continue Boyd's Artist Development Program. Like other Artistic Directors before him, he chose to steer the Company in a new direction, which in years to come will add another dimension to the history of the creative process within the RSC.

When considering an RSC pedagogy, I cannot speak for the current department since I retired in 2014, but during my years with the Company, I perceived that the pedagogy of text was firmly based on Berry's principles with strong traditional influences from Barton; however, the voice work was more difficult to define and reflected the diversity of the team, but above all, it was actor-responsive.

Stephen Kemble trained as an actor at Rose Bruford College, studied as a voice coach at Central, and is a qualified Linklater practitioner who has worked extensively at the RSC. He commented on the notion of an RSC pedagogy[16]:

It's difficult to think in terms of there being a pedagogy of voice at the RSC in that there is no one systemized way of approaching text and voice. The pedagogy is subtle, discreet, fluid, and emerges from the process of the work. There can be shifts almost project by project or company by company. It's influenced of course by the core practices of the coaches but also by the previous training and experience the actors bring both as individuals and as a group. This speaks to the core difference between voice teaching and coaching. Additionally, the director's views/visions/concepts for the productions may also affect the way the voice and text work are applied. The over-arching ambition and requirements from the Company's artistic leadership will again contribute to the "climate" of how voice and text sits within the company ethos. There are also strong traditions embedded in the life of the RSC, notably of course from Berry and Barton, and individual practitioners working now will feel a responsibility, maybe even a duty to honor these. Practitioners who have previously worked in the Company and who have subsequently published their own form of this work as they have experienced it will also have contributed to the view of "RSC voice and text." Many students and actors have derived their understanding of the work from these books in different contexts outside the work of the company. In short, there are many pedagogical influences at play that contribute to the voice and text work and which ensure that it does not become a fixed way of transferring knowledge, techniques or skills. (personal communication, May 2018)

Over the years, many defining theatre-voice practitioners have spent time at the RSC and gone on to influence actor training and theatre-voice practice worldwide. It is the responsibility of a funded company and a requirement of the RSC Royal Charter that it commits to progressing the theatre arts (Royal Charter of the Royal Shakespeare Company 1925, 2 II [3]). It is in the field of voice that the requirements have been met most fully. From 1875 to 2014, there was evidence of support for the development of voice and text skills for members of the acting companies and emerging practitioners. That the pedagogy evolved and responded to trends in theatre training community is testament to the vision and leadership of the Company's artistic directors. The influence of voice practitioners who have been part of the RSC voice and text journey, especially (but not solely) Cecily Berry and John Barton have enriched the theatre-voice community worldwide through public workshops, publications, and video recordings and support of amateur theatre groups and education initiatives.[17]

Notes

1. Portions of this article were originally a part of the doctoral dissertation called "Artist Development and Training in the Royal Shakespeare Company" (Darnley 2013).
2. In this article, the RSC will also be called "the Company."
3. This article uses an autoethnography methodology. It is "a form or method of research that involves self-observation and reflexive investigation in the context of ethnographic field work and writing" (Maréchal 2010, 43). The article uses personal communication with colleagues during my time at the RSC and offers a literature review of those figures concurrently. Chang (2009) outlines this practice and shows its use in histography. Holmes (2016) reflects on the application in voice training.
4. Evidence appears in archive material including an article in the *Stratford Herald*, November 10, 1876 (Sanderson 1984) and a statement by Charles Lowndes, Secretary of the Shakespeare Memorial Association entitled *Object of the Association, with Lists of Subscriptions*, Christmas 1877 (Lowndes 1877).
5. The Meiningen Company was active in Europe between 1874 and 1890 and established a reputation for a system of training and operation that could be described as early ensemble. Its influence on European ensemble theatre was considerable.
6. Rudolf Steiner's approach was both sensory- and movement-based. His approach stemmed from a belief that the nature of human speech and communication was fundamentally spiritual rather than merely concerned with meaning (Steiner (1924) 1959).
7. Byam Shaw was an actor turned director who became the director of the Old Vic Theatre School between 1947 and 1951. The school and the Young Vic Theatre was run by George Devine who was also an actor and director. The school formed part of Michel Saint-Denis' Old Vic Theatre Centre. All three resigned in 1951 after disagreements with the Board. Byam Shaw then became Quayle's co-director of the SMT in Stratford in 1952 before taking full charge from 1956 to 1959.

8. In 1993, Edgar Wreford produced copies of carefully notated lessons and described his work with Iris Warren in detail. The fact that he had found the classes highly beneficial was obvious from his enthusiasm about the work and since he had kept the copies of his notes for over 20 years. Wreford trained at the Old Vic School was a member of the Young Vic Company, The Birmingham Rep, and the Old Vic. In later years, he went on to teach and direct in drama schools. He died in January 2006 aged 82, and his obituary appeared in *The Stage*, February 8, 2006.

9. Cicely Berry has written books that have influenced actors, directors, voice teachers, and teachers in mainstream education. Her seminal publications include *Voice and the Actor, Your Voice and How to Use It, The Actor and the Text, Text in Action, Working Shakespeare Library*, and *Word Play: A Textual Handbook for Directors and Actors*. Berry was the first voice teacher at the RSC to publish her work for a wider audience, and her books have been influential on voice teaching worldwide ever since.

10. The Method is a common term for an acting technique based on the work of Konstantin Stanislavski and developed at the Group Theatre in New York City.

11. Voice teaching and coaching has always been a predominately female occupation and continues to be so, although more males are entering the profession. The reasons for this are complex and deserve full consideration elsewhere. Suffice to say that Berry was committed to developing a more gender-balanced team and appointed David Carey and later Andrew Wade to work with her. Both are recognized as master teachers in the field and have gone on to make significant contributions to the profession.

12. An intimate theatre spaced owned by the RSC.

13. The RST is the larger main house where the majority of Shakespearean productions are staged.

14. At this time, I had been appointed Head of Voice. This pilot program in 2003/2004 delivered training as workshops, classes in large or small groups, lectures for the entire group, or production-related research work for each cast member. More detailed information on the RSC Artist Development Program can be found in Darnley (2013), which includes the notes I made as a participant observer.

15. Capoeira is a Brazilian martial art that combines elements of dance and music.

16. Stephen Kemble is an experienced voiceover artist and teacher. He is co-author of *The Voiceover Book* (Hodge and Kemble 2014).

17. The headshot photo credit is Ellie Kurtz.

Disclosure statement

No potential conflict of interest was reported by the author.

Dedication

I dedicate this article to the memory of Cicely Berry and John Barton and to the rich legacy they left us.

References

Addenbroke, David. 1974. *The Royal Shakespeare Company, The Peter Hall Years*. London: Kimber.

Alford, Geraldine. 1963. "Memorandum." Studio Report – First Phase, May 6 – August 3. Maurice Daniels Collection, Shakespeare Centre Library, Stratford-upon-Avon, UK.

Barton, John. 1984. *Playing Shakespeare*. London: Methuen.

Beauman, Sally. 1982. *The Royal Shakespeare Company: A History of Ten Decades*. Oxford: Oxford University Press.

Berry, Cecily. 1992 [1987]. *The Actor and the Text*. London: Virgin.

Berry, Cecily. 1998. "Forum." Presented at the National Theatre Studio *Verse Speaking and Classical Text*, London, October 30.

Brockbank, Philip, ed. 1985. *Players of Shakespeare 1: Essays in Shakespearean Performance*. Cambridge: Cambridge University Press.

Brook, Peter. 1963. "What About Real Life?." In *The Crucial Years*, Edited by Royal Shakespeare Company. Stratford-upon-Avon, UK: Shakespeare Centre Library and Archive, pp. 2–3.

Carey, David. 2003. "Interviews with Patsy Rodenburg and Cicely Berry." *Voice and Speech Review* 3 (1): 227–235. doi:10.1080/23268263.2003.10739407.

Chambers, Colin. 2004. *Inside the Royal Shakespeare Company: Creativity and the Institution*. London: Routledge.

Chang, Heewon. 2009. *Autoethnography as Method*. London: Routledge.

Cribb, T. J. 1999. "Obituary: George Rylands." *Independent*, January 20. https://www.independent.co.uk/arts-entertainment/obituary-george-rylands-1075032.html.

Darnley, Lyn. 2013. "Artist Development and Training in the Royal Shakespeare Company." PhD diss., University of London.

David, Hodge, and Stephen Kemble. 2014. *The Voiceover Book*. London: Oberon Books.

Denne Gilkes Memorial Fund. 2018. "About Denne Gilkes." Accessed November 2. https://www.dgmf.co.uk/about-denne-gilkes.

Endowment Scheme. 1923. Stratford-upon-Avon, UK: Shakespeare Centre Library and Archive.

Fogerty, Elsie. 1934. "Letter to Archie Flower, July 12." Archibald Flower Correspondence, Shakespeare Memorial Theatre 1928–1940. Stratford-upon-Avon, UK: Shakespeare Centre Library and Archive.

Ganong, Joan. 1962. *Backstage at Stratford*. Toronto: Longmans.

Hodge, Alison, ed. 2000. *Twentieth Century Actor Training*. London: Routledge.

Holmes, Shannon. 2016. "Autoethnography and Voicework." *Voice and Speech Review* 10 (2–3): 190–202. doi:10.1080/23268263.2016.1337552.

Jones, Nicholas. 2000. "Discussion of Michael Boyd's 1999 *A Midsummer Night's Dream*." Presented at the Barbican Theatre, London, February 18.

Linklater, Kristin. "Vocal Traditions: Linklater Voice Method." *Voice and Speech Review* 12 (2): 211–220. doi:10.1080/23268263.2018.1444558.

Lowndes, Charles. 1877. *Object of the Association, with Lists of Subscriptions*. Stratford-upon-Avon, UK: Shakespeare Centre Library and Archive.

MaGuiken, Aislinn. 2000. "*Henry VI* Company Discussion." Presented at the Clapham Rehearsal Rooms, London, February 22.

Maréchal, Garance. 2010. "Autoethnography." In *Encyclopedia of Case Study Research*, edited by Albert J. Mills, Gabrielle Durepos, and Elden Wiebe, 43–45. Vol. 2. Thousand Oaks, CA: Sage.

Marshall, Lorna, and David Williams. 2000. "Peter Brook, Transparency and the Invisible Network." In *Twentieth Century Actor Training*, edited by Alison Hodge, 174–190. London: Routledge.

Merlin, Bella. 2001. *Beyond Stanislavisky*. London: Nick Hern Books.

Michael, Boyd. 2003. "Discussion." Presented at the Ensemble Acting Company, Royal Shakespeare Company, London, December 8.

Noble, Adrian. 2002. "Letter Outlining Changes." May 25. Stratford-upon-Avon, UK: Royal Shakespeare Company. doi:10.1044/1059-0889(2002/er01)

Parker, Kate. 1985. "Goodbye, Voice Beautiful." *Plays and Players* 382: 32–34.

Quayle, Anthony. 1990. *A Time to Speak*. London: Barrie and Jenkins.

Rose, Clifford. 1963. *Report on Verse Speaking Tutorials. Stratford-upon-Avon*. UK: Shakespeare Centre Library and Archive.

Royal Charter of the Royal Shakespeare Company. 1925. "Orders of the Privy Council, March 6." London: Privy Council.

Royal Shakespeare Company. 2002. "Appointment of Michael Boyd as RSC Artistic Director Press Release." *Press Release*. Stratford-upon-Avon, UK: Shakespeare Centre Library and Archive. doi:10.1044/1059-0889(2002/er01)

Rudlin, John. 2000. "Jacques Copeau: The Quest for Sincerity." In *Twentieth Century Actor Training*, edited by Alison Hodge, 52–76. London: Routledge.

Saint-Denis, Michel. 1962. *Memorandum to Hall, Brook Donnell, and Patrick Donnell, September 10. Maurice Daniels Collection*. Stratford-upon-Avon, UK: Shakespeare Centre Library and Archive.

Saint-Denis, Michel. 1963. "Three Men Look Ahead." In *The Crucial Years*. Edited by Royal Shakespeare Company. Stratford-upon-Avon, UK: Shakespeare Centre Library and Archive. pp. 7–8.

Saint-Denis, Michel. 1982. *Training for the Theatre: Premises and Promises*. London: Arts Books.

Sanderson, Michael. 1984. *From Irving to Olivier: A Social History of the Acting Profession in England 1880–1983*. New York: St. Martin's Press.

Selbourne, David. 1982. *The Making of A Midsummer Night's Dream*. London: Methuen.

Steiner, Rudolf. 1959 [1924]. *Speech and Drama*. London: Anthroposophic Press.

Trowbridge, Simon. 2003. "Stratfordians: A Dictionary of the RSC". Accessed 2 November 2018. www.stratfordians.co.uk

A Historical View of the Pedagogy of Public Speaking

Erika Bailey

ABSTRACT
This article offers a short history of the pedagogy of public speaking. Beginning with the Greek's creation of the field of rhetoric, the article follows the development of the teaching of public speaking in the Roman era, the European Middle Ages, and Renaissance, and then the article focuses on public speaking in America through to the present day. This article traces the development of public speaking from its more formal and declamatory roots in rhetoric and oratory to the more personal, conversational style used in the wake of the introduction of radio and television. The teaching of public speaking has also necessarily shifted over time in terms of where speaking skills have been taught (within formal educational systems or without), how accessible speaking training was and to whom, and how formalized the rules of correct performance have been. The article ends with a discussion of current trends in public speaking and whether there may be more space in public speaking pedagogy for the robust civic dialogue so strong in nineteenth century America.

Introduction

In this article I aim to sketch a brief history of the pedagogy of public speaking. Public speaking is a broad subject and has a history as long as community itself, a history tied tightly to political and linguistic developments. To narrow the focus somewhat, I will look at the history of the field within the western world, starting from the Greeks and Romans then staying in Europe through the Middle Ages to Renaissance England, and then to the United States during the Civil War period through the present day. I have lingered on particular elements of this history that I felt would be of greatest interest and use to voice and speech trainers, following developments in ideas on the vocal and physical performance of public speech more faithfully than the writing of public speeches, for example. I have been particularly intrigued by the constant balancing of focus in training between the content and style of public communication and where this balance might move in the future.

Classical Rhetoric

"Public speaking" as a term was not used until the eighteenth century (Sproule 2012, 563) and not until the early twentieth century did it denote the conversational style in use today by speakers. Prior to the eighteenth century (and for a time after) public speaking (as it is known

---

today) was studied and written about under the banner of rhetoric. Aristotle (384–322 BCE) defined rhetoric as the art of "discovering in any particular case, all of the available means of persuasion" (Corbett and Connors 1999, 1). From its origins, then, public speaking was an interaction between audience and speaker with the aim of moving the audience's opinion in one direction or another. The first records of a formalized system for shaping public address begin with stories from the fifth century BCE in Sicily. Here a tyrant, Thrasybulus, was overthrown and in order to regain property lost under his rule, citizens had to argue in court (Corbett and Connors 1999). Corax formulated a system to aid citizens in creating successful arguments for the return of their property and the advice he systematized formed the bedrock of rhetoric. Roughly a hundred years later, Aristotle's (384-322 BCE) writings on rhetoric became the first foundational text on the subject. It is good to note that the origin story for rhetoric occurs in a community exploring more democratic forms of government. As citizens began to have opportunities to speak up, methods and rules for public argument were created. Training groups of people in oratory and public speaking is unnecessary in societies where very few are allowed to speak in public. As Brian Vickers (1998) writes in his *In Defence of Rhetoric*, "In a democratic society, with free speech and due recognition of the individual's rights to being represented in legal and political activities, rhetoric has a real role to play" (214).

Its origins were in the courtroom, but Aristotle's writings and teachings on rhetoric also gave guidelines for political and ceremonial speech and as the field developed over centuries it could be said to cover almost all forms of communication from marketing, to letter writing, to fiction as well as the more traditional arenas for rhetoric in law and politics. Several hundred years after Aristotle, Cicero (106 BCE-26 CE) would categorize rhetoric into five major subject areas: *Invention* which suggested methods for finding the most persuasive argument on any given subject; *arrangement*, where speakers would organize arguments into an effective order; *style*, which explored word choice and phrasing, creating an elevated or more colloquial feel to the argument; *memory*, which concerned methods of memorization, and *delivery*, which covered vocal and physical aspects of performance (Bailey 2011). Over the course of its history, rhetoric would become a field of study of written persuasion but at its origins, before printing presses, public communication happened through the spoken word and rhetoric was the study of oral communication.

From the very first writers on rhetoric and oratory, a long-standing tension in the field emerged. Plato (424–348 BCE) did not approve of rhetoric:

> Rhetoric could not be considered a true art because it did not rest on universal principles. Moreover, rhetoricians, like poets, were more interested in opinions, in appearances, even in lies, than in the transcendental truth that the philosopher sought [...] they were mere enchanters of the soul, more interested in dazzling their audience than in instructing it. (Corbett and Connors 1999, 492)

Aristotle was Plato's student but a strong defender of rhetoric. Plato's argument was that rhetoric was a performance that aimed to play on the emotions of an audience and win them over rather than a deeper search for philosophical truth. Plato's criticism was particularly aimed at a group of itinerant teachers of rhetoric referred to as the Sophists who he and others accused of training young statesmen of the day in eloquence above truthfulness. Aristotle countered Plato's argument, stating that a masterful rhetorician must use logic and reasoning as well as an awareness of an audiences' probable emotional response, and must also be a good person, an *ethical* person using ethical arguments (DeCaro 2011). This tension between the substance of speech and the style in which it was shared has continued in communication studies to the present day.

While Corax was the first teacher of rhetoric named in the history books, Isocrates (436-338 BCE) was the first Greek to create an established school of rhetoric and oratory. His model of rhetorical education was successfully replicated many times throughout the region and through these schools, rhetoric quickly became central to Greek education (Vickers 1998). Greek orators then travelled to Rome, and over the next several centuries Romans developed the field further. While there is a lack of specific examples of Greek rhetorical education, by the second century BCE there are sources that can give us a sense of the education Roman students would have received (Heath 2014). Scholars of the period have used copies of classroom lectures, handbooks of rhetorical principles, and texts with demonstration materials to sketch a picture of the activities within a Roman classroom:

> Beginners worked on a graded series of introductory exercises that familiarized them with a number of techniques that would need to be combined in a complete speech (e.g. telling a story, criticizing or defending a narrative's plausibility, arguing a general thesis). [...] Students would then proceed to the more advanced exercise [...] in which they were given a hypothetical scenario and asked to speak on one or the other side of a judicial or deliberative dispute arising from it. (Heath 2014, 9)

From here students were taught how to organize and arrange their arguments and how to explore style and word choice to create different effects. Rhetoricians notated dozens of sentence structures that they labeled "schemes" and "tropes" such as parallelism, metaphor, personification, and syllogism. Students had to memorize each of these devices, notate their use in speeches they studied, and use them in speeches they wrote themselves. An education in rhetoric was flexible, allowing preparation for arguments in law or politics, and for any number of points of view. The skills were organizational and structural rather than content specific.

Middle Ages and Renaissance

In the wake of rising Christianity in the Middle Ages, Greek and Roman culture disintegrated. Many of the pivotal rhetorical texts disappeared during this time or survived only in damaged fragments (Vickers 1998). Nevertheless, rhetoric remained central to educational philosophy. Rhetoric, grammar and logic comprised the *trivium*, the four-year course of study for undergraduates in Europe during the Middle Ages. Logic, however, was considered the most important aspect of that education (Corbett and Connors 1999), and the field of rhetoric became a course of study in delivering sermons (for those embarking on a life in the church) and mere letter writing for the lay student. Certainly, the Middle Ages was not a time rife with possibility for public discourse and persuasion. "The disappearance of the face-to-face, persuasive context of rhetoric meant that rhetoric theorists lost sight of the audience" (Vickers 1998, 227) and the field as a whole became somewhat anemic during this era.

The Renaissance was not only a rebirth in literature, scientific research, art forms, and intellectual explorations, but it was also a rebirth in an active use of rhetoric through the rediscovery of many key Greek and Roman rhetorical texts. In England, the Renaissance began in the late 1400s, and rhetoric was key to the emerging richness of English Renaissance literature. In the early 1500s Erasmus, a humanist scholar, and John Colet, the Dean of St. Paul's Cathedral, both wrote reforms of secondary education that guided the curriculum of many of England's grammar schools (St. Paul's, Eton, Winchester, Westminster) for generations (Vickers 1998).[1] In an effort to create students who were fluent in Latin, familiar with Latin literature, and in full command of every rhetorical figure and trope named in the history of rhetoric, students were taught small morsels of information or vocabulary daily. They would be required to repeat the master's explanation, memorize it, and then recite it. They would review the information the next day and then review all of the new lessons at the end of the week (Vickers 1998). As students advanced, they were expected to use the figures of speech in their own writing and speaking, and they were expected to be able to recite the passages they had memorized for years after first learning them. This intense process of memorization and recitation had a large impact on the written and spoken language of the time:

> Credit for the ability of so many Renaissance writers to use the full expressive resources of language must be given to the humanist school-system and to the masters who so energetically enforced it. As we can see from their later compositions, the schools exerted a lasting impression on the writers who attended them [such as Shakespeare, Marlow and Ben Jonson]. (Vickers 1998, 264)

This rhetorical system of education may be credited with creating great writers, and specifically great writers of the spoken word. Little is written about the great orators of the Renaissance, which is in contract to the wealth of information about the great orators in the classical eras. The tightly hierarchical governance of the Renaissance left little room for public argument. Nevertheless, there are a number of great Renaissance dramatists, who wrote intricate, muscular language to be spoken aloud. This richness of spoken language may be due to the particular intensity of language education that these writers experienced.

The Elocutionary Movement

As rhetoric moved into the seventeenth and eighteenth centuries, it developed philosophically, aesthetically, and practically (DeCaro 2011). I will focus on the elocutionary movement that arose at this time as the other developments veered from what would be considered the roots of contemporary public speaking. The elocutionary movement reached its zenith in the mid 1700s and focused primarily on delivery rather than invention and arrangement (DeCaro 2011). Due to an increasing middle class in England and America during the eighteenth century, a growing number of professionals needed public speaking skills. This era was, therefore, hungry for lessons on delivery and performance. The newly minted middle class had access to advice on public speaking skills through public lectures and increasingly available printed books.

Thomas Sheridan (1719–1788), an Irish actor and educator, was the most well-known writer and thinker of the elocutionary movement. He earned a BA and an MA from Trinity College in Dublin and then went on to become an actor and playwright before taking on a career as a teacher of elocution. Sheridan's most representative book, *Lectures on Elocution* was written in1762 and "deals exclusively with the problems of delivery—articulation, pronunciation, accent, emphasis, tone, pause, pitch, voice control, and gesture" (Corbett and Connors 1999, 514). The book is a compilation of seven of his very popular lectures (Mahon 2001, 67). Sheridan's work was hugely popular and was influential enough to receive honorary degrees from Oxford and Cambridge, but he has also always been viewed critically, both in his own time and in more recent assessments. Phillippa Spoel (2001), in her article *Rereading the Elocutionists*, quotes historian Wilbur Howell as saying:

> The elocutionists made rhetoric appear to be the art of declaiming a speech by rote, without regard to whether the thought uttered were trivial or false or dangerous; and under auspices like these, rhetoric became anathema to the scholarly community. (49)

This focus on delivery and lack of critical attention to the material itself, make sense coming from a former actor whose job was to interpret and perform scripts rather than to rewrite them or argue them. This conflict between content and style, between training speakers to focus on what is being said as opposed to how it is being said mirrors the conflict between Plato and Aristotle. As with Plato's attack on the Sophists, here we see strong criticism levied against a school of thought with a stronger focus on delivery than on invention and arrangement, to use traditional names of topics more associated with content.

Nineteenth Century America

In 1776, the American colonies had seven colleges; but by 1850 there were over 400 colleges in the United States, and rhetoric was taught at most of them (Corbett and Connors 1999). Increasingly, however, a class on rhetoric focused on methods of persuasive writing as opposed to persuasive speaking. At Harvard University in 1806, John Quincy Adams, then a United States Senator, became the first Boylston Professor of Rhetoric. He lectured on political speech, an activity he practiced daily in his duties as a Senator. Subsequent, professors who held this title slowly shifted the study of rhetoric away from oral to written address and then to the less persuasive and more aesthetic communications of fiction and poetry. Once again, as in the Middle Ages, some form of rhetoric remained an integral part of higher education, but a practical study of public speaking could no longer be discovered on a university campus (Heinrichs 1995). While academia lessened its focus on public speaking, primary education and adult education gave the American citizen of the nineteenth century many opportunities to improve his (and now possibly her) skills in public communication.

Rhetoric had been an integral part of formal education since the Greeks, yet the percentage of people who received a formal education had been fairly small. This began to change in the United States in the nineteenth century as more of the population had access to primary education, which included public speaking. According to Urban and Wagoner (2013), by 1870, every American state had public elementary schools funded by tax dollars. Even earlier than this, by 1840, around 55% of American children between 5 and 15 attended public or private schools. Access to schooling depended significantly on race, gender, and geography (with black children being legally barred from receiving any type of education in many states before the Civil War), but an increasingly large percentage of young white Americans, boys and girls, began to go to school.

The McGuffey Readers were some of the most widely used texts in elementary education in the United States. Over 120 million copies of these readers were sold between 1836 and 1960 (Boorstin 1973), and presumably more than 120 million students used the books. Only the Bible and Webster's Dictionary sold more copies during that time. The readers were a series of graded textbooks that shared poems, stories, essays, and speeches in order to teach students reading skills, vocabulary acquisition, and, importantly, public speaking. "It is sometimes forgotten that these books, out of which generations of American schoolchildren learned to read, aimed to teach boys and girls how to read *aloud*" (Boorstin 1973, 463). During the nineteenth century, school children were graded and advanced in school based on their ability to read aloud correctly. Recitation and declamation exercises were common activities in and out of the schoolroom during this time (Boorstin 1973). Not only did the books contain increasingly difficult reading material for students to comprehend and analyze, but lessons were also provided in pronunciation and articulation. In effect, these books made every American schoolteacher a public speaking and elocution teacher as much as a reading teacher. The skills of speaking well and correctly were integral to taking part in civic and professional life in nineteenth century America.

Engagement with public speaking often continued long after individuals finished their elementary education. Small and large towns across the country hosted lectures, debates, and amateur dramatics often sponsored by local lyceums. Lecturers and entertainers would travel the lyceum circuit. The Lyceum Movement "dominated the organization of community lectures and the training of orators in the nineteenth century" (Foner and Branham 1998, 2). Outside of the formalized structure of the Lyceum Movement, local citizens themselves would organize and perform debates and lectures as a form of community entertainment and educational advancement. The speaking that occurred by amateurs and professionals in these public realms was governed by a set of rules regarding pronunciation, diction, and resonant sound. These rules were partly in place because public speaking, especially to larger audiences, required full sound and detailed articulation in order to be heard and understood by large crowds. These rules of elocution, however, also conveyed social status and proof that the speaker was worthy of a listen. "Oral articulateness had a social capitol, which it no longer does for us" (McWhorter 2011, 43). Many of these rules of correct pronunciation and formal address were followed well into the twentieth century.

If ordinary middle class citizens were embracing oratory and elocution, any individual wishing to take a leading part in the political life of the country was doubly required to model elaborate diction and full resonance. This was a rich era in public speaking as it combined the need for full and expressive voice use, an aspect of all oral cultures, with an admiration for complexly structured language that can only be mined in a society where access to written language is honored and taken for granted. "When the youthful William Jennings Bryan's 'Cross of Gold' oration won him the presidential nomination at the Democratic National Convention in Chicago in 1896, the popular awe for great orations in the bombastic style was confirmed" (Boorstin 1973, 466). This style, ornate in its use of language and in its use of vocal flourish and diction, would not survive long into the twentieth century.

Public Speaking for Women and African-Americans

Until this point in the traditional history of public speaking in the western world, the major players had all been educated white men. In American history, white women and women and men of color had thus far been largely excluded from access to the pulpit, the soapbox, and the podium. White men with means had access to education, professions, and the organizational infrastructure that gave them opportunities to speak to groups of people. Women and men of color were excluded from these spaces as speakers but often as audience members as well. This started to change in nineteenth century America. A number of popular social movements such as the temperance movement, suffrage, and importantly, the abolition movement gave opportunities for white women and women and men of color to address diverse gatherings.

Women's public speaking, when even marginally acceptable, was circumscribed by topic and audience. "Gender was a major social division in the nineteenth century, and women were allowed the greatest opportunity to speak when they addressed only women rather than speaking to mixed gender, 'promiscuous' audiences" (Bean 2006, 23). While it was frowned on for women to speak publicly, it was somewhat more acceptable for them to speak on subjects concerning piety, charity, and sympathy (Bean 2006). Temperance, education and the abolition movement were therefore acceptable subjects. Women began to lecture on these subjects in the lyceum circuit in the decades prior to the Civil War. The opportunity to speak regularly gave women valuable speaking experience, which had been scarce prior to this century. These growing skills proved invaluable as the fight for suffrage continued.

For African-Americans, the abolition movement created a groundbreaking opportunity for public speech in mixed race spaces. Prior to this, according to Watts et al. (2001), "the very act of black speaking (and writing) was subject to severe censure [...] African American orators were often beaten and killed for attempting to exercise the liberty of free speech" (87). With the explosion of anti-slavery activity that took place in the 1830s, African-American orators began to speak to white audiences for the first time (Foner and Branham 1998), which was in and of itself a revolutionary act. Black orators had to be careful, however, in the subject and manner in which they addressed white audiences:

> When former slaves such as [Frederick] Douglass sought to move beyond autobiographical narratives to broader considerations of politics and social prejudice, they often met opposition from their presumed allies. Douglass was advised by [...] colleagues not to sound too "learned" because people might not "believe you were ever a slave" (Foner and Branham 1998, 6).

Thankfully, these restrictions were not in place for African-Americans when addressing their own communities. By the nineteenth century, African-Americans already had a long history of oratory and public speech much of it centered around black churches. These communities "conferred extraordinary importance upon the development and use of oratorical skills as a means by which to achieve both social reform and individual advancement" (Foner and Branham 1998, 2). Vernon Jordan, former head of the National Urban League, gives a sense of the pedagogy of public speaking within the black community in the introduction to a collection of his speeches. Jordan was born in 1935, so his education was decidedly twentieth century, but his introduction gives a sense of the traditions that might have been present in the late nineteenth century:

> My interest in public speaking came very early. It began in St. Paul African Methodist Episcopal Church, in Atlanta, with the children's Easter Sunday afternoon program. The children of the Sunday school were asked to give a memorized presentation, usually a combination of scripture and religious poetry on the theme of Easter [...] We attended Easter practice several times a week, and then, come Easter Sunday [...] the congregation [...] assembled to hear us. All children got their applause. Even children who cried, stumbled, or remained silent out of fear [...] were applauded [...] I intuitively understood that speaking well was highly valued. The very roots of the African Methodist Episcopal (AME) Church and other black denominations sprang from blacks determination to be able to speak freely, passionately, and persuasively [...] I had a rich diet of speakers to listen to at St. Paul [...] I understood that first, the speaker had to lay a good foundation, to give you his text and subject, to tell you what he was going to talk about. Then, in the middle part of the speech I looked for information and inspiration; even at a young age, I rejected volume and fireworks. Finally came the crescendo and the conclusion. How could I know all this as a young boy? It was all intuitive; I could feel it. (Jordan 2009, xii-xv)

While Jordan writes of intuiting the skills necessary to speak persuasively, he paints a picture of a community actively creating experiences for young people to listen analytically to speakers and to explore speaking in public from a young age. He describes speaking memorized texts written from stirring language, and he narrates an experience of listening critically to many powerful speakers, noting the structure and style of their oratory. Classical and Renaissance students of rhetoric engaged in these very same activities of memorized speaking and careful analysis. African-Americans raised in this tradition were able to take well-honed speaking skills into mixed race audiences to fight for abolition, suffrage and later civil rights.

The nineteenth century was one of expanding educational and speaking opportunities for an increasingly diverse group of people. The preferred speaking style of the time was formal: robust in sound and ornate in diction. Communities gathered in halls and churches across the country to listen to speakers address the issues of the day, which included humanitarian causes and scientific discoveries. The sound and style of speech, the subjects of public discussion, and this form of community gathering all changed quickly at the beginning of the twentieth century.

Twentieth Century America

The biggest changes to the field of public speaking were caused by the technological advances that revolutionized communication in the twentieth century. Home telephones were increasingly in use by the early 1900s (Boorstin 1973), and radios arrived in people's homes in the 1920s:

> When the only way to address thousands was from a platform, the formal, oratorical mode had been inevitable: the speaker had to stand up, shout loudly, and make broad gestures in order to be understood in the far corners [...] Radio changed all this [...] Both speaker and listener found themselves in a new locale, which made possible a new relationship [...] "public speaking" became just talking. (Boorstin 1973, 470)

Radio announcers began to create a new, more informal mode of public address that American politicians took to emulating. By 1933 Franklin Delano Roosevelt was welcomed into American homes through the radio for a "fireside chat" not a stirring oration.

As this more intimate, personal style of communication developed, it spread beyond the radio and beyond politicians into daily commerce and education. Radio also helped to blur the lines between entertainment, education, and advertisement. Dale Carnegie (1888–1955) arrived in the midst of these changing modes of communication to teach the American population how to navigate the new speaking world. Carnegie moved to New York City from Missouri and in 1912 began teaching a course in public speaking at the YMCA. In 1936 he published the still famous *How to Win Friends and Influence People*. His students wanted to "develop poise and self-confidence. They wanted to get ahead in business" (Boorstin 1973, 468). His courses grew in popularity until he began to train others how to teach his classes. Ultimately, he franchised his system, which was subsequently taught throughout the country. In 1970 over 1.5 million people enrolled in a Dale Carnegie public speaking class (468). The transformation in public speaking between Bryan's "Cross of Gold" speech in 1896 and the methods Carnegie shared was dramatic, "from the models and standards of "eloquence" and "oratory" to the person and his problems, from "elocution" and "declamation" to self-improvement and personal success. Carnegie had a list of six ways to make people like you:

(1) Become genuinely interested in other people.
(2) Smile.
(3) Remember that a person's name is (to that person) the sweetest and most important sound in any language.
(4) Be a good listener, encourage people to talk about themselves.
(5) Talk in terms of the other person's interest.
(6) Make the other person feel important, and do it sincerely. (Boorstin 1973)

While intellectuals and the literati looked down on this philosophy, as they had looked down on Sheridan and the Elocutionists 200 years earlier, and as Plato had looked down on the Sophists in an earlier era, millions of Americans found it useful and applicable. Much of this advice may sounds familiar to public speaking students today, who may hear similar instructions from contemporary teachers. The other major change this kind of Carnegie-inspired language reveals is the growing focus on the audience in public speaking training. "In a sense the shift is from speaker centered (How good a performer are you?) to audience centered (How well do you engage your audience for a purpose?" (Keith and Lundberg 2014, 141). It is a shift from a stirring solo performance to a persuasive conversation. Dale Carnegie's winning, self-improvement philosophy, in the wake of revolutionary changes in communication technology, ultimately begins this transition to more contemporary styles of public speaking.

This new style was part of a growing business culture in the United States, and the style of speaking within that culture became a dominant mode of expression beyond the business world. Colleges now had practical public speaking classes in the early and mid-twentieth century. The lyceum movement had ended in the wake of radio and television entertainment, but extracurricular speaking opportunities also continued to increase for young Americans, black and white. Intercollegiate debating societies existed in most colleges, complete with coaches and frequent tournaments (Boorstin 1973). The Improved Benevolent Protective Order of Elks of the World, one of many African-American civic organizations, held oratory competitions that Thurgood Marshall, Maya Angelou, Martin Luther King Jr., and Oprah Winfrey all participated in (Taylor 2017; McWhorter 2011). Public speaking skills were seen as equalizing, as a way for Americans of all backgrounds to improve themselves and to climb the ladder of success.

The values and style of public speaking that Dale Carnegie articulated are still in use today. Expectations of formality of speech in public settings have continued to relax and the importance placed on personal connection with the audience has continued to be vital. Access to modes of public communication continues to expand through proliferating cable channels and the internet. While following the rules of formal elocution may no longer be the key to proving a speaker's merit, one might argue that the quality of visual aids such as PowerPoint in presentations has become another public speaking skill to master in order to be taken seriously. Ted Talks with their intelligent, sympathetic and casual style, with the clear aim of improving the audience's day to day lives, may be seen as a direct development from Carnegie's pragmatic training. The last contemporary trend I would like to highlight is the great value currently placed on personal stories from public speakers, rather than objective, non-partisan points of view which held greater value in previous generations. This has led to a different mode of *invention*, to return to the classical rhetorical term—a different series of steps to find persuasive arguments. Students are now asked to learn public speaking through a series of exercises that highlight their unique experiences. Unlike previous generations of public speakers, today's speech makers are rarely asked to memorize or imitate the style of other individual speakers. As I looked over several classes on public speaking offered to Harvard students, the exercises described in course materials ask students to generate their own content after examining various styles of communication. Some of the prompts might be to "create a speech to teach" or "to change an opinion," a ceremonial speech, or an impromptu speech. Classical rhetorical pedagogy would have had students create and present their own speeches, but only after a deeper immersion in the canonical literature that often included extensive mimetic training. This seems an entirely appropriate shift in a current American culture (I assert) that values new ideas and experimentation above repetitive learning, and that is captivated by the individual subjective experience above illusive objectivity.

Reflection on the Future

As I look back through this history of public speaking, I am particularly drawn to the pre-Civil War era. Indeed, the style could be bombastic, and the standards for correct speech and elocution were exclusionary and hierarchical. Nevertheless, it was an era when greater numbers of people were gaining access to audiences and were speaking on issues vital to their communities and to the survival of the country as a whole. It could be argued that it is at times of growing inclusion that rules of correct behavior proliferate. Those rules can be exclusionary, but they can also be guide posts to people new to a field. The conversational style of presentations that has been developed through the twentieth century has provided us with more connection between audience and speaker, and thoughtful, nuanced moments of public communication, lacking in previous eras, but at the same time, I feel something has also been lost. Keith and Lundberg (2014) in their article "Creating a History for Public Speaking Instruction" argue that teachers of public speaking "ought to recover and return to the civic and humanistic mission of public speaking pedagogy" (139) that we have found in previous eras.

Certainly, good public speaking instructors have always asked students to bring their beliefs and passions into the classroom and find a persuasive way to share them. In looking over the broad expanse of public speaking history, however, it is clear that the moments when the pedagogy of communication has focused more narrowly on delivery and presentation technology over and above the substance and ethical implications of speaking, have been the moments when public speaking as a field has been critiqued and trivialized. I feel we are at a moment where we can reinvigorate impassioned, well -researched, ethical public speaking. While practical public speaking classes are popular with students at colleges and universities, they are often undervalued by faculty and the institutions themselves. If we think of the rich civic history of the field of public speaking, however, of the skills it has given lay people to argue in court, to challenge unjust laws, to elect representatives, to argue for the abolishment of slavery, to win votes for disenfranchised citizens, as well as to ace an interview and secure funding for a new organization, then we might see more of the vital, even revolutionary, possibilities in a course on public speaking. Foner and Branham (1998), in their anthology of African-American Speeches *Lift Every Voice*, assert that for nineteenth century Americans, "to learn to speak well oneself was to prepare for participation in civic life and reform" (1). I find this an inspiring challenge—can we make public speaking classes places to train students to become members of a community, a community they have the possibility of changing for the better through their words and voices. We might see a public speaking class as a place where we can teach interview techniques and the simplicity and refinement of presenting a Ted Talk, but the classes may also give students the opportunity to practice speaking with the passion and power that Emma Gonzalez employed at the March for Our Lives rally.[2] We need articulate, persuasive, and ethical speakers at this moment in our country's history, and our public speaking classrooms may be the place where those speakers can practice taking a breath, grounding themselves, and lifting their voices.

Notes

1. In the United Kingdom, a grammar school is a term for a traditionally elite college preparatory school. Often, these schools emphasized a classical education, teaching Greek and Latin languages and literature.
2. See Emily and Cruz (2018) for more information about this speech.

Disclosure statement

No potential conflict of interest was reported by the author.

References

Bailey, Erika. 2011. "Classical Rhetoric and Heightened Text: Creating an Introductory Class for Actors." *Voice and Speech Review* 7 (1): 55–65. doi:10.1080/23268263.2011.10739520.

Bean, Judith Mattson. 2006. "Gaining A Public Voice: A Historical Perspective on American Women's Speaking." In *Speaking Out: The Female Voice in Public Contexts*, edited by Judith Baxter, 21–39. New York: Palgrave Macmillan.

Boorstin, Daniel J. 1973. The Americans: The Democratic Experience. New York: Random House.

Corbett, Edward P. J., and Robert J. Connors. 1999. *Classical Rhetoric for the Modern Student*. New York: Oxford University Press.

DeCaro, Peter A. 2011. "Origins of Public Speaking." In *Public Speaking: The Virtual Text*, accessed 9 July 2018. http://www.publicspeakingproject.org/PDFS/chapter2.pdf.

Emily, Shapiro, and Wil Cruz. 2018. "Emma Gonzalez Brings March for Our Lives Rally to an Emotional Silence." *ABC News*, March 24. http://abcnews.go.com/US/emma-gonzalez-brings-march-lives-rally-emotional-silence/story?id=53988048

Foner, Philip S., and James Branham, eds. 1998. *Lift Every Voice: African American Oratory, 1787–1900*. Tuscaloosa: University of Alabama Press.

Heath, Malcolm. 2014. "Rhetoric and Pedagogy." *The Oxford Handbook of Rhetorical Studies*,73-85, doi:10.1093/oxfordhb/9780199731596.013.005.

Heinrichs, Jay. 1995. "How Harvard Destroyed Rhetoric." *Harvard Magazine* 97 (6): 36–42.

Jordan, Vernon. 2009. *Make It Plain: Standing up and Speaking Out*. United States: Public Affairs.

Keith, William, and Christian Lundberg. 2014. "Creating a History for Public Speaking Instruction." *Rhetoric and Public Affairs* 17 (1): 139–146. doi:10.14321/rhetpublaffa.17.1.0139.

Mahon, M. Wade. 2001. "The Rhetorical Value of Reading Aloud in Thomas Sheridan's Theory of Elocution." *Rhetoric Society Quarterly* 31 (4): 67–88. doi:10.1080/02773940109391215.

McPhail, Mark, Robert E. Lawrence, Eric Terrill, King Watts, and Kirt H. Wilson. 2001. "African American Rhetoric." In *Encyclopedia of Rhetoric*, edited by Thomas O. Sloane. Oxford: Oxford University Press.

McWhorter, John. 2011. *Doing Our Own Thing: The Degradation of Language and Music and Why We Should, Like, Care*. New York: Random House.

Spoel, Philippa M. 2001. "Rereading the Elocutionists: The Rhetoric of Thomas Sheridan's. A Course of Lectures on Elocution and John Walker's Elements of Elocution." *Rhetorica: A Journal History of Rhetoric* 19 (1): 49–91. doi:10.1525/rh.2001.19.1.49.

Sproule, J. Michael. 2012. "Inventing Public Speaking: Rhetoric and the Speech Book." *Rhetoric and Public Affairs* 15 (4): 563–608.

Taylor, Alexis. 2017. "Elks Hold National Convention in Baltimore." *Afro: The Black Media Authority*, August 9. https://www.afro.com/elks-hold-national-convention-baltimore-2/.

Urban, Wayne, and Jennings Wagoner. 2013. *American Education: A History*. 5th ed ed. New York: Routledge.

Vickers, Brian. 1998. *In Defence of Rhetoric*. Oxford: Clarendon Press.

Watts, E., Wilson, K., McPhail, M., & Terrill, R. (2011). African-American rhetoric. In (Ed.), Encyclopedia of Rhetoric. :Oxford University Press,. Retrieved 22 June. 2018, from http://www.oxfordreference.com.ezp-prod1.hul.harvard.edu/view/10.1093/acref/9780195125955.001.0001/acref-9780195125955-e-4.

Historical Landmarks in Singing Voice Pedagogy

Matthew Hoch

ABSTRACT

This article provides a brief overview of some of the most seminal and important events in the history of singing voice pedagogy, from the earliest historical writings through the most recent twenty-first century developments. Topics include primary sources from the Renaissance through the romantic eras; an exploration of bel canto concepts and methodologies; reflections on figures such as Manuel García II, William Vennard, Ralph Appelman, and Richard Miller; the history of professional organizations in the United States and their role in shaping scholarly discourse in voice pedagogy; the revelation and influence of acoustic theory, vocology, and contemporary commercial music (CCM) pedagogy in recent decades; and a look at the pedagogical horizon in the coming decades. Readers are provided with additional resources for further study.

Introduction

This article provides a brief overview of some of the most seminal and important events in the history of singing voice pedagogy. While the list, like any list, is subjective—the inclusion of some topics over others is endlessly debatable—the following are certainly landmark moments and essential emergent themes that are worthy of discussion and reflection.

Although we start at the beginning with a brief survey of historical writings for the voice, the article places greater emphasis on the modern era, particularly the twentieth century, which witnessed some of voice pedagogy's greatest revelations as technology and scientific knowledge of the voice rapidly evolved. Some of the latter topics are illustrations of current trends that have received much scholarly attention in the early twenty-first century. The article will conclude with speculation on what the future may hold for singing voice pedagogy.

It should be noted that—due to the survey nature of this article—all of these topics are, to an extent, incomplete discussions. Each one of these topics could have been expanded into a book in its own right (and many have been). Important names, resources, and topics will not be mentioned simply due to the confines of this short article. It is my hope that the reader interested in delving more deeply into any one of these topics consult the many resources that are listed in the endnotes and bibliography.

One final comment should be made. This article focuses exclusively on the canon of Western music. The discipline of singing voice pedagogy—as it has been shaped by treatises, traditions, conferences, and professional organizations—has its roots in European classical music. Although pedagogies for various types of world music certainly exist, they are both outside the scope of this article and the expertise of the author.

The Recorded Beginnings: Tosi and Other Early Writers

It is difficult to pinpoint the beginnings of voice pedagogy, but it is safe to say that humans have been singing since prehistoric times. The thinkers of the Ancient Greek world, such as Plato (427–347 BCE) and Aristotle (384–322 BCE), wrote of the importance of singing as part of a complete humanistic education (Sell 2005, 186). Likewise, the Judeo-Christian writings of the Tanakh/Old Testament also include passages in the books of Exodus, Judges, 2 Chronicles, and Ecclesiastes, and—most important—the 150 Psalms of David that are intended to be sung.[1] Soon after the establishment of the early Roman Catholic Church, an official "school of singing" (presumably a choir school) was founded by Pope Sylvester (285–335) in Rome for the purpose of training young singers for liturgical services. Thus, voice pedagogy must have existed in some form, but unfortunately, there are no writings that have been preserved from this era that outline the specifics of pedagogic strategy or approach.

During the Renaissance, however, selected pedagogic works begin to appear in writing. Horst Günter (1997) proposes that the first book on singing was the German scholar Conrad von Zabern's de *modo cantandi choralem cantum* in 1474 (Miller [1977] 1997, 9–12). Karen Sell (2005) and Richard Miller (2017), in their attempts to survey the early history of singing voice pedagogy, also list Franchinus Gaffurius (1451–1522), Bénigne de Bacilly (1625–1690), Maffei (fl. 1562–1573), Zacconi (1555–1627), and Giulio Caccini (c. 1545–1618) as important early figures. Nicola Porpora (1686–1756) was perhaps the most important singing teacher of the early eighteenth century, but unfortunately, he wrote little. Porpora's reputation rests almost entirely upon his outstanding legacy of successful pupils, including the castrati Caffarelli (1710–1783) and Farinelli (1705–1782) as well as the female sopranos Regina Mignotti (1722–1808) and Catarina Gabrielli (1730–1796).

Most discussions concerning the early history of voice pedagogy begin with discussion of Pier Francesco Tosi (c. 1653–1732). Tosi was an Italian castrato, composer, and writer of music. He is best known for his early treatise on singing, *Opinioni* de' *cantori antichi, e moderni* (1723), which is one of the first voice pedagogy treatises to have been preserved in its entirety. In 1743, twenty years after it was first written, the treatise was published in English as *Observations on the Florid Song*. Still available in print, Tosi's work is especially valuable for its catalog of various baroque ornaments utilized by singers at the time. This tendency to focus on style, execution, and the literature as opposed to confronting vocal technique and voice production directly is a hallmark that spans most of the earliest treatises on singing voice pedagogy. Tosi was also primarily concerned with castrati. He is, however, the most agreed upon starting point for scholars of historical voice pedagogy.

For many years, the most reliable anthology of historical documents related to voice pedagogy was Berton Coffin's *Historical Vocal Pedagogy Classics* (1989). This book influenced an entire generation of singing teachers interested in exploring historical pedagogy. It is no accident that Coffin begins with Tosi's treatise; he then proceeds onward to Giambattista Mancini (1714–1800), Manuel García I (1775–1832) and his son, Manual García II (1805–1906), Mathilde Marchesi (1826–1913), Julius Stockhausen (1826–1906), Enrico Delle Sedie (1822–1907), Francesco Lamperti (1811–1892) and his son, Giovanni Battista Lamperti (1839–1910), and Lilli Lehmann (1848–1929). Some of these figures will be discussed later in this article.[2]

Bel Canto Traditions

One of the most ubiquitous terms in voice pedagogy is *bel canto*, which literally means "beautiful singing" in Italian. *Bel canto*, however, is a broad concept that is difficult to grasp in large part due to the multifarious nature of the definition itself. The term is at once an aesthetic concept and tonal preference (which varies according to context and style period), a reference to flexible and florid singing, a specific operatic repertory, and a school of voice pedagogy. In addition, *bel canto* can mean different things depending on the social-historical context of the time period in question. In my 2014 book, *A Dictionary for the Modern Singer*, I attempted to confront this complexity as concisely as possible by defining *bel canto* as follows:

> ***bel canto***. (1) An Italian phrase meaning "beautiful singing," referring to a flexible, coloratura style of singing. In this sense, *bel canto* was used to describe the florid operas of George Frideric Handel (1685–1759), the arias from which showcased the virtuosity of the singer. The same phrase was used to describe florid singing in later eras of Italian opera as well.
>
> (2) A label for the specific brand of Italian opera that emerged at the beginning of the nineteenth century in Italy, featuring florid-style singing and legato Italian melodies. Gioacchino Rossini (1792–1868), Gaetano Donizetti (1797–1848), and Vincenzo Bellini (1801–1835) represent the apotheosis of the genre. Many of Giuseppe Verdi's (1813–1901) operas retain elements of the *bel canto* school of Italian opera.
>
> (3) A school of voice pedagogy roughly equivalent to the International Italian School. While the specific tenets that define *bel canto* pedagogy can be somewhat ambiguous—and vary widely from teacher to teacher, all of whom may claim to subscribe to *bel canto* ideals —a practical definition assumes a reverence to the treatises and method books of the great Italian pedagogues, with an emphasis on the central canon of Italian operatic repertoire. Some pedagogues have defined the *bel canto* school of pedagogy more narrowly, for instance, Lucie Manén, in her 1987 treatise, *Bel Canto*. (Hoch 2014, 24)

While there are literally hundreds of introductions to *bel canto* concepts—both historical and contemporary—one of the most impactful single-volume resources is James Stark's 1999 book *Bel Canto: A History of Vocal Pedagogy*. In this work, Stark offers an in-depth exploration of the historical schools of voice pedagogy over the course of 300 pages. Toward the conclusion of his book, he includes an essay entitled "*Bel Canto*: Context and Controversy," which discusses how the term *bel canto* has meant different things to different singers, pedagogues, and eras. Stark synthesizes this multitude of meanings into his own definition of *bel canto* as follows:

> *Bel canto* is a concept that takes into account two separate but related matters. First, it is a highly refined method of using the singing voice in which the glottal source, the vocal tract, and the respiratory system interact in such a way as to create the qualities of *chiaroscuro*, *appoggio*, register equalization, malleability of pitch and intensity, and a pleasing vibrato.[3] The idiomatic use of this voice includes various forms of vocal onset, *legato*, *portamento*, glottal articulation, crescendo, decrescendo, *messa di voce*, *mezza voce*, floridity and trills, and *tempo rubato*.
>
> Second, *bel canto* refers to any style of music that employs this kind of singing in a tasteful and expressive way. Historically, composers and singers have created categories of recitative, song, and aria that took advantage of these techniques, and that lent themselves to various types of vocal expression. *Bel canto* has demonstrated its power to astonish, to charm, to amuse, and especially to move the listener. As musical epochs and styles have changed, the elements of *bel canto* adapted to meet new musical demands, thereby ensuring the continuation of *bel canto* in our own time. (Stark 1999, 149)

Stark attempts to crystalize *bel canto* by exploring various topics through primary sources, including the *coup* de *glotte*, *chiaroscuro*, registration, *appoggio*, vibrato, and ornamentation, and he succeeds as masterfully as anyone reasonably can.[4] His exhaustive approach, however, reveals how difficult it is to define *bel canto* as a cohesive vocal technique. Perhaps no one stated this as directly as Richard Miller, who in *The Structure of Singing* writes:

> Why not just put ourselves in the hands of someone who teaches "The old *bel canto* method" and be done with it? We cannot because there is no specific codified system of *bel canto* waiting for the vocal neophyte to pick up and assimilate. Despite some claims that certain teachers have a direct link to "the old Italians," no modern teacher can honestly profess to teach some clearly delineated method that is universally recognized as being "the *bel canto* method."
>
> Anyone who has studied with teachers who trace a historical lineage to other persons often cited as major teachers of *bel canto* (for example, pupils of pupils of Giovanni Battista Lamperti) must admit that the specifics, the actual techniques of acquiring the art of beautiful singing, are only imprecisely enunciated by them. A careful reading of the pedagogical literature of the historical *bel canto* period must lead to a similar conclusion. The term *bel canto* has become a twentieth-century *shibboleth*, with opposing methodologies staking out highly suspect claims for its possession. This is because of the indefinability of the term beyond its literal meaning: beautiful singing. Skills of sustaining and moving the voice (*cantilena* and *fioritura*) are required to execute the *bel canto* literature; those skills join to produce "beautiful singing." They call for the most exacting technical accomplishments, in whatever century. (Miller 1986, xx–xxi)

In spite of Miller's apparent cynicism, there are actually many hallmarks of *bel canto* within the "International Italian School" for which he so passionately advocates. It was Miller, more so than any single figure who contributed to the trove of historic *bel canto* writings, who distilled a cohesive, systematic approach in *The Structure of Singing*. However, this kind of prescribed, formulaic approach to technique was not part of the conscious agenda of the Italian *bel canto* masters. Rather, broader concepts were. Perhaps no Italian master was more influential upon twentieth-century American voice pedagogy than Lamperti, who wrote the following to his pupil William Earl Brown at the conclusion of his studies with Lamperti in Dresden in 1893:

The mantle of my father, Francesco Lamperti, fell upon me. It now descends to you, for you have grasped the truth of the Old Italian School of Singing, which descended from the Golden Age of Song, by word of mouth. It is not a method. There is no "bell canto" [sic] system of teaching. Mental, physical, and emotional reactions are the fundamentals of this old school." (Brown 1931, 127)

Bel canto pedagogy should not be thought of as something that is merely historical. *Bel canto* traditions—now labeled by many, thanks to Richard Miller, as the "International Italian School" of voice pedagogy—persisted throughout the twentieth century and into present day practice. In the twenty-first-century, scientifically informed or "fact-based" singing teachers coexist somewhat peacefully alongside those who identify as old-fashioned teachers from the *bel canto* tradition, and still more singing teachers draw from both traditions in their pedagogy.

While scientific singing voice research—mostly acoustic and biomechanical—tends to dominate present day singing conferences, most significantly the annual Voice Foundation and PAVA symposiums and the biennial NATS conference, there is still a vibrant (if less robust) community of scholars still interested in the significance of historical pedagogy. Perhaps the most important scholar who has contributed to this field is Stephen F. Austin, Professor of Voice at the University of North Texas. His regular column, "Provenance," has appeared in the *Journal of Singing* regularly since 2004, comprising an extensive repository of writings on various aspects of historical pedagogy.[5] Other excellent resources include recent writings by Daniela Bloem-Hubatka (2012) and Michael Trimble (2013).

Methodologies: Skill-Acquisition-Based Pedagogy

During the nineteenth century, various methodologies for the voice exploded. These graduated "practice books" established themselves in singing studios and were used throughout most of the twentieth century, although their ubiquity seems to have waned considerably in recent decades. Many performers, particularly of more experienced generations, were raised on vocalises by Nicola Vaccai (1790–1848), Giuseppe Concone (1801–1861), Henrich Panofka (1807–1887), and Mathilde Marchesi (1821–1913), to name four of the most famous examples of methodology composer-authors.

A method book, by itself, is not a comprehensive approach to vocal technique. Virtually none in this nineteenth-century tradition are unaccompanied by any kind of prose explanation of *appoggio*, registration, *messa di voce, coup* de *glotte*, or any other core *bel canto* concept.[6] Rather, it is up to the teacher to apply context, explanation, and —most important—technical advice when working with the student through these progressive exercises. The primary purpose behind a methodology is skill acquisition, particularly skill acquisition that works toward the goal of singing a very specific repertory: nineteenth-century Italian *bel canto* repertoire. In other words, the goal of a methodology is the successful execution of the literature. In and of themselves, they do not attempt to unravel the mystery of vocal function.

Other important authors of nineteenth-century methodologies include Franz Abt (1819–1885), Pasquale Bona (1808–1878), Giovanni Marco Bordogni (1789–1856), Adolphe-Léopold Dannhauser (1835–1896), Louis Lablache (1794–1858), Francesco

Lamperti (1811–1892), Giovanni Battista Lamperti (1839–1910), Bernhard Lütgen (1835–1870), Salvatore Marchesi (1822–1908), Auguste Mathieu Panseron (1796–1859), Gioacchino Rossini (1792–1868), Giovanni Battista Rubini (1794–1854), William Shakespeare (1849–1931), Ferdinand Sieber (1822–1895), Max Spicker (1858–1912), and Pauline Viardot (1821–1910).[7]

Manuel García II: The Dawn of the Modern Era

James Stark (1999) writes the following about the Manuel García II's unique position in the history of singing voice pedagogy:

> If there was a single point in music history when the tradition and science of singing met, it was in the life and work of Manuel García II. Perhaps it would be more correct to say that with García, tradition and science not only met, but collided with a force that is still felt today. García was one of those seminal historical figures whose career marked a watershed between the past and the future. An heir of the old Italian school of singing, at the same time he belonged to a generation of scientific minds who wished to look beyond the mere appearance of things to their underlying ideas. (4)

Thus, García *fils*—to distinguish him from his father, the great Rossini tenor García *père* or García I—marks the beginning of the march toward a twentieth century, anatomical understanding of the singing voice. His achievements in voice pedagogy are manifold, and his primary contributions to the discipline are twofold: the concept of the *coup* de *glotte* ("stroke of the glottis"—a unnecessarily but inevitably complex discussion topic that is beyond the scope of this article) and his writings, particularly the treatise *Hints on Singing* (1894).

In spite of these achievements, the contribution for which García II is perhaps most famous is the invention of the laryngoscope in 1854.[8] For García, this early laryngoscope was essentially a mirror attached to the end of a stick so that the vocal folds could be observed indirectly. García, after many observations of his own larynx, published his findings in *Observations of the Human Voice* in 1855, the first laryngological publication of its kind. He quickly developed a reputation throughout Europe as a teacher of injured voices, and he was famously credited with restoring the voice of Jenny Lind (1820–1887), the "Swedish Nightingale."

Interestingly, García's work was viewed with derision in many circles of the singing world, particularly the old-school *bel canto* community, who had little interest in physiologic function and saw it as too drastic a departure from "golden era" approaches to the voice. I am inclined to think that this scorn was due in large part to García II's place within his famous singing family. His father, Manuel García I, was a student of Porpora and one of the most famous tenors in Europe. His many roles included Almaviva in Rossini's original 1816 production of *Il barbiere di Siviglia*. In addition, Manuel's two sisters were the world-class mezzo-sopranos Maria Malibran (1808–1836) and Pauline Viardot (1821–1910). Naturally, a major career was expected of Manuel García *fils* as well, but it was not to be. After several false starts, he retired from singing and went about his pedagogic endeavors.

Perhaps this status as the only "non-singer" alongside such esteemed kinship contributed to García II's mixed legacy. Thankfully, García *fils*'s reputation has aged well—no history of singing voice pedagogy would be complete with substantial discussion of his unique legacy.

The Birth of Professional Organizations

Formal professional organizations for singing teachers were largely a twentieth-century phenomenon. The first organization for singing teachers in the United States was the New York Singing Teachers Association (NYSTA), which was established in New York City in 1906. First named the National Association of Teachers of Singing, the organization acquired its current name officially in 1917.[9] NYSTA's origins were firmly grounded in the teachings of the Italian *bel canto* tradition. The original ten-member board of directors numbered five known exponents of Manuel García II, Pauline Viardot-García, or one of their students. In the second year of incorporation, NYSTA concerned itself with examinations and certification for singing teachers, holding public meetings to foster discussion and debate. This effort to establish standards was directed under the leadership of the first chairman, Herman Klein. A prodigious author, editor, and voice teacher, Klein had the *imprimatur* of Manuel García who remarked in a published letter: "It is gratifying to me to know that the great American people appreciate the sound theories of the old school, and they will assuredly find in you one among its few capable exponents" (Shigo and Ohrenstein 2006, 6–7). NYSTA's professional development program, which was founded many years later by Oren Lathrop Brown (1909–2004), is still at the very heart of the organization's mission, delivering core courses in vocal anatomy and physiology, voice acoustics and resonance, vocal health for voice professionals, singer's developmental repertoire, and comparative voice pedagogy. *VOICEPrints*—the journal of NYSTA—is published five times annually.

The world's largest association of singing teachers, the National Association of Teachers of Singing (NATS), was founded in 1944. Unlike NYSTA, which remained a local organization for the tristate area throughout the entirety of the twentieth century, NATS was founded with national ambitions. By the twenty-first century, NATS membership had grown to more than seven thousand. The association's members primarily come from the United States and Canada, but twenty-five other countries are also represented. NATS hosts biennial national conventions, and student auditions occur at the chapter, regional, and national levels. The NATS Intern Pro- gram, a prestigious mentoring program for young teachers of singing, is also offered each summer. *The Journal of Singing*—the official publication of NATS—is published five times annually.

Founded in 1969 in New York City by the physician Wilbur James Gould, the Voice Foundation brings together physicians, scientists, speech-language pathologists (SLPs), performers, and teachers to share their knowledge and expertise in the care of the professional voice user. The mission of the Voice Foundation is to enhance knowledge, care, and training of the voice through educational programs and publications for voice care professionals and public and professional voice users, and through supporting and funding research. Since 1972, the Voice Foundation has sponsored an annual symposium entitled "Care of the Professional Voice." This interdisciplinary academic conference is a showcase for the most current and cutting-edge voice research not only in the country, but the world. "Voice Pedagogy Sunday," which occurs on the last day of the symposium, is a favorite among singing teachers. Since 1989, the Voice Foundation has been led by Robert Thayer Sataloff, an internationally renowned otolaryngologist who is also a professional singer and conductor, as well as author of more than 600 publications, including more than thirty-six textbooks.

International Congress of Voice Teachers (ICVT) began convening in 1987. It is not a professional organization per se, but rather a consortium of professional organizations from all over the world that now gathers once every four years. The first nine ICVT events were held in Strasbourg, France (1987); Philadelphia, United States (1991); Auckland, New Zealand (1994); London, England (1997); Helsinki, Finland (2001); Vancouver, Canada (2005); Paris, France (2009); Brisbane, Australia (2013); and Stockholm, Sweden (2017). The next congress will be held in Vienna, Austria, in 2021.

The Pan-American Vocology Association (PAVA) is a membership-driven group of voice professionals from all voice-related vocations including vocologists, SLPs, physicians (otorhinolaryngology), professional singers, singing teachers, voice and speech trainers, and voice therapists. PAVA is an association, not a foundation, with elected officers whose terms rotate every two years according to a set of bylaws. In this sense, the organization combines the interdisciplinary nature of the Voice Foundation with a governance structure that is more similar to NATS. The mission of PAVA is to advance the scientific study of voice for artistic and professional use by fostering vocology in all countries of the Western Hemisphere through research, dissemination of knowledge, training, and the creation and development of professional standards and credentialing in voice habilitation.

Conferences held by the four organizations mentioned above—PAVA, NATS, ICVT, and (especially) the annual Voice Foundation Symposium—have been quintessentially important in uniting the profession, increasing interdisciplinary studies, disseminating scientific research, and exploring new lines of pedagogic inquiry. There are also numerous other professional organizations, conferences, summer workshops, and symposia emerging each year, so many that one cannot possibly keep up with all of the opportunities that are available. The impact of professional organizations on late-twentieth and twenty-first-century voice pedagogy cannot be overstated. They have firmly established themselves as an integral part of the modern pedagogic landscape.

Vennard, Appleman, and the Dawn of a Fact-Based Era[10]

The year 1967 heralded the dawn of a new "fact-based" era in voice pedagogy.[11] This is almost entirely due to the publication of two seminal textbooks in the history of singing voice pedagogy: D. Ralph Appelman's *The Science of Vocal Pedagogy: Theory and Application* and the revised and enlarged (and definitive) version of William Vennard's *Singing: The Mechanism and the Technic*. The appearance of these two books in the same year revolutionized undergraduate and graduate voice pedagogy classes in universities across the United States for the next two decades. Vennard's book was particularly ubiquitous, enduring for almost twenty years until Richard Miller's landmark *The Structure of Singing* was published in 1986.

Like many seminal events in intellectual history, the timing was right for the appearance of these two books. The profession not only was ready for them, it needed them. In the latter half of the twentieth century, a fundamental shift occurred as our knowledge of voice science increased, clarifying aspects of vocal function and demystifying many aspects of singing and the teaching of singing. While some myths were debunked, many tenets of traditional *bel canto* teachings that had worked for centuries were validated by modern science.

Thus, modern singing pedagogues often divide voice pedagogy into two eras, a historical era that was followed by a fact-based one as knowledge of science increased. There is a strong argument to cite 1967 as the dividing line between these two eras due to the publication of Appleman's and Vennard's treatises, both of which are firmly grounded in anatomy and physiology and focus on vocal function. This emphasis on vocal function—as opposed to imagery or other historical approaches—is an essential feature of fact-based era pedagogy.

While the works of D. Ralph Appelman and William Vennard might seem dated today, their importance in the history of American voice pedagogy cannot be overemphasized. Both *The Science of Vocal Pedagogy: Theory and Application* and *Singing: The Mechanism and the Technic* reflect pedagogic truth as they—and the profession— understood it in 1967, and much of what they wrote is still remarkably relevant. Most important, the developments in voice pedagogy that would occur throughout the 1970s, 1980s, 1990s, and 2000s could not have occurred without their pioneering work.

Acoustic Theory: Sundberg, Coffin, and Contemporary Figures

In virtually all contemporary voice pedagogy courses and textbooks, there is substantial discussion of the basic acoustics of the singing voice. Even many undergraduate music majors now understand the concept of formants. This was not always the case, however, and acoustic theory is actually a rather recent development in singing voice pedagogy. Although Peterson and Barney (1952) published their pioneering article in the *Journal of the Acoustical Society of America* as early as 1952, and although Vennard ably touched on the topic in 1967, it would not be until the 1970s and beyond that the common singing teacher began to seriously wrestle with formants and their implications when teaching vowels, registration, and tone quality.

In 1977, *Scientific American* published a definitive article by Johan Sundberg (1977) on vocal acoustics. In the words of Jeannette LoVetri, Sundberg:

> discovered that classical singers' voices exhibit a certain amount of consistency in terms of both physiologic response and acoustic parameters. These hallmark characteristics are some of the ingredients classical singers need to acquire, either through training or by natural tendency, or both, if they are to succeed at the highest levels. (as quoted Hoch 2014, 210).

Sundberg would eventually publish *The Science of the Singing Voice* (1989), which would become the essential "bible" of acoustic theory for an entire generation of singing teachers.

Berton Coffin (1910–1987) was also an early pioneer with a more practical approach. Unlike Sundberg, who is a voice scientist first and foremost, Coffin was a singing teacher with an interest in voice science. Although he authored many publications, his most important two books were *The Sounds of Singing: Vocal Techniques with Vowel-Pitch Charts* (Coffin [1976] 1987)) and *Overtones of Bel Canto: Phonetic Basis of*

Artistic Singing with 100 Chromatic Vowel-Chart Exercises (1980). His most famous pedagogic tool was a "chromatic vowel chart" that, when spread across the piano keyboard, advocated systematic vowel modification in various parts of the vocal range to achieve resonance via scientific and acoustic principles.

Contemporary voice pedagogy resources—such as Scott McCoy's *Your Voice: An Inside View* (McCoy [2004] 2012)—have become increasingly masterful at simplifying the concept of formants for students and teachers of singing. In the second decade of the twenty-first century, Ken Bozeman's two books—*Practical Vocal Acoustics* (2013) and *Kinesthetic Voice Pedagogy* (2017)—have been greeted with sincere enthusiasm by the broader singing community. Acoustic theory is no longer a topic reserved for PhD students; these are basic concepts now understood by an increasing majority of singing teachers. In 2016, Ian Howell published his theory on Absolute Spectral Tone Color (ASTC), a revolutionary concept that is certain to generate considerable discussion as acoustic theory enters its next decade of research.

Richard Miller: The Formulation of a Systematic Approach

In 1998, Richard Miller (1926–2009) wrote that "the influence of the Lamperti maxims [have] never been surpassed by other pedagogic writing in the twentieth century."[12] I argue that the influence of Lamperti's maxims have perhaps been surpassed only by the writings of Miller himself. Miller is arguably the most prolific and important modern classical voice pedagogue, and inarguably one of the most influential among North American singing teachers. More modern singing teachers affirm Richard Miller's ideas than any other single pedagogue.

Miller's landmark 1986 treatise, *The Structure of Singing*, introduced a systematic approach to voice pedagogy that is still widely in practice among singing teachers. Miller's long career as a singing teacher was spent almost entirely at the undergraduate institution of Oberlin College in Oberlin, Ohio. There, he founded the Otto B. Schoepfle Vocal Arts Center, one of the first vocology laboratories in the United States dedicated to studying the singing voice. In addition to *The Structure of Singing*, Miller wrote many other books, the most important of which is *National Schools of Singing* (Miller [1977] 1997)), the result of hundreds of hours of observing singing lessons in England, France, Germany, and Italy. Miller concluded that the "International Italian School" was the most physiologically practical approach to singing, particularly emphasizing the importance of *appoggio* breath management.[13]

The Structure of Singing dissects vocal technique according to function and into the specific subsystems of respiration, phonation, resonance, and articulation, prescribing specific exercises for various aspects of singing technique. Miller's paradigm is organized according to the following categories (the numbers indicate chapters in *The Structure of Singing*):

1. Onset and Release
2. Breath Management
3. Agility/Flexibility
4. Resonance
5. Vowel Balancing

6–7.   Resonance (nasal and non-nasal consonants)
8.   *Sostenuto*
9–10.   Registration (male and female)
11.   Vowel Modification
12.   Range Extension
13.   *Messa di voce* and Dynamic Control
14.   Vibrato and Vocal Timbre
15–17.   Extra-Technical Concerns

In many ways, Miller's approach is an augmentation of the skill-acquisition-based approach of many of the *bel canto* methodologists, who prescribed exercises assigned to sequentially develop specific aspects of vocal technique (and with the intent of singing—both in their case and in Miller's case—classical vocal repertoire). Miller, however, goes far further than his predecessors by thoroughly annotating each set of exercises with lengthy prose, detailing the physiology at work behind the technique. This decoding of vocal technique—making the invisible if not visible, at least more understandable—is *The Structure of Singing*'s most important contribution to the pedagogic literature.

Miller's systematic approach revolutionized voice pedagogy over the course of the next two decades, uniting the profession. His impact was especially felt among academic singing teachers; the groupthink of the NATS community is still very much in the Miller lineage, especially among classical singing teachers. In the coming years, new pedagogic works by Barbara Doscher ([1988] 1994), Clifton Ware (1998), and Scott McCoy ([2004] 2012) would become important descendants of the systematic, fact-based approach to singing that was advocated by Miller, carrying his concepts into the twenty-first century.

Vocology: The Science and Practice of Voice Habilitation

The term vocology entered the lexicon relatively recently in the history of voice pedagogy. Vocology was first coined in conversation in 1988 between Ingo Titze, a voice scientist at the University of Iowa, and George Gates, an otolaryngologist at Washington University in St. Louis. It was then introduced at a conference in 1989 by Gates and published in an article by Titze the following year (1990). Titze and Gates defined vocology as "the science and practice of voice habilitation" and viewed it as a discipline that would parallel audiology. Audiology, the branch of science that studies hearing, balance, and related disorders, is a well-established field with a long history behind it. Vocology, however, is much newer as a systematic discipline. Vocology is perhaps even more interdisciplinary in nature, involving voice scientists, speech-language pathologists, ENTs, and voice practitioners.

The most significant ways in which vocology parallels audiology is the emphasis on one major organ (ear versus larynx) and acoustic-mechanical-electrical energy transduction. One could devise the following respective academic and professional definitions:

Audiology (A):   The study of hearing
Audiology (P):   The diagnosis and treatment of hearing disorders

Vocology (A):   The study of vocalization
Vocology (P):   The science and practice of voice habilitation

In addition, both (at least in recent years) have respective professional organizations:

> *American Speech-Language-Hearing Association (ASHA)*
>
> *Pan-American Vocology Association (PAVA)*

It should be noted that "habilitation" is distinct from the related term, "rehabilitation." They are not interchangeable. Whereas voice *rehabilitation* specialists (speech-language pathologists) help to restore injured voices to normal function, *habilitative* specialists (vocologists, singing and acting voice teachers), train healthy voices to do extraordinary things. Habilitate means to enable, equip, or capacitate. Titze makes the following observations:

> Voice habilitation is more than repairing a voice or bringing it back to a former state, even if that state may have been judged statistically as normal; rather, it is the process of strengthening and equipping the voice to meet very specific and special demands. [...] Asking a stock trader at the New York Stock Exchange, or a coach along the sidelines of a basketball court, to "hold down" the voice is like telling a boxer not to get hit or a ballerina not to get on her toes (Titze 1990, 21).

Exceptional vocal skills, according to Titze, may include the following: (a) Loudness and pitch ranges beyond normal conversational speech; (b) duration of vocalization beyond a population norm; (c) amplified versus unamplified voice for professional and recreational needs; (d) voice quality variations, including the use of multiple sound sources; (e) voice impersonation, mimicking, disguise, accent training; and (f) high-effort vocalization (shouting, screaming, calling, and other "primal sound" making).[14]

Perhaps Titze's greatest contribution to the contemporary singing voice teacher is the research on and the inclusion of semi-occluded vocal tract (SOVT) exercises in the practice regimen. The most popular SOVT exercise used by singing teachers is what many call "straw phonation" (singing through a straw as part of a warm up or technical exercise. In the following passage, Titze both defines SOVT exercises and explains the science behind them:

> My team and others around the world have discovered, scientifically, the merits behind various different voice therapy techniques. They can be all covered with one phrase called "semi-occluded vocal tract" methods. What we mean by that is, in order to make the vocal folds function in the most efficient way, one needs to practice with the mouth almost closed. So we do exercises like lip trills, or making a sound through a thin straw. I have a video on YouTube explaining straw phonation. It has been viewed by close to one hundred thousand people now. There are other varieties of semi-occluded vocal tract exercises, such as tongue trills and hums. Some people promote water bubbling with a straw. All of these techniques have one thing in common: They create a pressure in the oral cavity that helps to set the vocal fold into their ideal position. The nearly closed tube also helps to create a feedback so that the acoustic pressures in the mouth help to drive the vocal folds, increasing the efficiency of the sound production. That to me has been a most significant discovery that reaches across speaking, singing, and every other kind of vocalization.[15] (communication on the "Voice Forum" Facebook group, July 3 2016)

In 2000, Titze founded the Summer Vocology Institute (SVI) under the auspices of the National Center for Voice and Speech (NCVS). SVI is a summer academy for vocology training, attracting singing and acting voice teachers, speech-language pathologists,

Table 1. Milestones in The History of Vocology.

1992	Specialty training track at the University of Iowa established
1994	Publication of *Principles of Voice Production* (Titze 1994)
1997	Journal: *Logopedics, Phoniatrics, Vocology* (Europe)
1998	Manual: "Guide to Vocology" (Verdolini)
2000	Summer Vocology Institute (SVI) founded
2005	Wikipedia entry (without trademark identity)
2012	*Vocology* textbook published (Titze and Verdolini Abbott 2012)
2013	Specialty Training in Vocal Health (STVH) symposium
2014	Pan-American Vocology Association (PAVA) founded

choral directors, and other voice professionals. The coursework consists of 9.0 graduate credits offered in three blocks over a period of eight weeks. The organization and credit distribution are as follows:

Block I: Principles of Voice Production (3.0 credits)
Block II: Voice Habilitation (2.0 credits)
            Instrumentation for Voice Analysis (2.0 credits)
Block III: Voice for Performers (2.0 credits)

The institute began in Denver (2000–2008) and is now located in Salt Lake City (2010–present). There are currently over 200 alumni teaching in universities and working at clinics all over the United States and internationally. Table 1 shows the chronological development of many vocology milestones.

Vocology is yielding important discoveries in voice research that has important implications for twenty-first-century singing teachers, and the nature of vocology—to habilitate the voice and facilitate exceptional voice use—has important implications for acting voice teachers and professional voice users as well.

Contemporary Commercial Music (CCM) Pedagogy

One of the most important developments in singing voice pedagogy that has occurred over the last several decades is the overwhelming acceptance of non-classical or con-temporary commercial music (CCM) styles into mainstream voice pedagogy.[16] As recently as the 1970s and 1980s, there was hardly anyone available to teach singing lessons that were not classical in nature. This is perhaps due to the training that singing teachers received—all university degrees were classical as well.

What is astonishing about this reality is that popular singing styles dominated virtually the entire twentieth century—on Broadway, on jazz records, and on radio and television. Why was this teaching style not being? Performers were left to figure it out on their own, sometimes avoiding classical singing teachers for fear of contaminat-ing their style with undesirable "classical" sounds or colors. There is a famous anecdotal story dating from 1930, when George Gershwin heard Ethel Merman sing "I Got Rhythm" for the first time. Enthralled by her robust belt voice, he asked:

Gershwin: "Ethel, do you know what you're doing?"
Merman: "No."
Gershwin: "Well keep doing it, and never go near a singing teacher."

This was probably excellent advice at the time, as it would take another forty years before specific pedagogies to deal with non-classical styles would begin developing. Perhaps it is not surprising that some of the earliest events in the history of CCM pedagogy occurred in and around New York City, which had long been established as the music theater capital of the world, as well as the home to a plethora of other CCM styles. Specifically, four seminal figures emerged as pioneers during the 1970s and 1980s: Jo Estill, Jeannette LoVetri, Seth Riggs, and Robert Edwin.[17]

It cannot be overstated that Robert Edwin was an extremely important figure— perhaps the most pivotal one—in convincing professional organizations like NATS to support other styles beyond classical singing. This was primarily due to his regular "Bach to Rock" column, which appeared in the *NATS Bulletin* and the *Journal of Singing* from 1985 through 2002. According to Edwin:

> In the early 1980s, Richard Miller was editor-in-chief of the *NATS Bulletin*, and he asked me to develop the first regular column dedicated to "nonclassical" voice pedagogy and repertoire. The "Bach to Rock Connection" debuted in the last issue of the *NATS Bulletin* in June of 1985 and continued to appear regularly for seventeen years in the *NATS Journal* from 1985 to 1995 and then in the *Journal of Singing* from 1995 to 2002. In 2002, I became an associate editor of the *Journal of Singing* and the column was retitled "Popular Song and Music Theater." That column continues to this day and—thanks to my colleague and friend Jeannette LoVetri—we now have a legitimate name for our work: contemporary commercial music (CCM) voice pedagogy rather than the vague and somewhat demeaning "nonclassical." (personal communication, May 26 2017)

In 1983, the New York Singing Teachers Association (NYSTA) hosted an event entitled the "Music Theater and Popular Music Symposium," which featured several presenters, including Oren Brown and Jo Estill. The symposium proved to be controversial to the establishment because the concept of "legitimizing" these nonclassical styles was alarming to many of the classical voice teachers who served on NYSTA's board of directors. According to Jeannette LoVetri, immediately after the symposium "the NYSTA board of directors met, and half of them resigned in protest because people were 'dragging the organization down' by promoting 'that' music, which was really just noise" (personal communication, May 15 2017). While there was obviously still much work to do, the first steps toward establishing CCM pedagogy as a bona fide discipline had been made.

Seventeen years would pass before the National Association of Teachers of Singing (NATS) would follow in NYSTA's footsteps. In 2000, NATS sponsored its first-ever "belting workshop" at the University of Miami. Norman Spivey and David Ward were the organizers, and presenters included Liz Caplan and Neil Semer, who were both teachers who lived and worked in New York. The success of this workshop led to a second one a year later, in 2001. This time, it was held in New York City. Neil Semer returned, along with Jo Estill, Jeannette LoVetri, and Mary Saunders Barton. By this time, the seeds of a new pedagogy were planted. With NATS finally supportive of exploring "nonclassical" styles, the road was paved for more progress to be made.

As Edwin mentions above, LoVetri's coining of the term "contemporary commercial music" represents another pivotal moment in the history of CCM pedagogy. According to LoVetri, she first began using this term around the year 2000 (personal communication, May 15 2017). The term first appeared in print three years later in a research paper by Jeannette LoVetri and Edrie Means Weekly (2003). In the early 2000s, several NATS chapters began offering annual music theater auditions alongside their classical ones, and eventually the national organization followed suit, encouraging these auditions. It is now unusual to find a NATS chapter that does not offer a music theater category at their student auditions. In 2014, with the inauguration of the National Student Auditions, national guidelines were established for both classical and music theater singers.

Four decades ago, no one could have predicted the presence and importance that CCM has achieved in the voice pedagogy community. Its flourishing as a discipline worthy of standing alongside classical singing has been steady and—recently—rapid, and advances in CCM pedagogy show no signs of slowing down. In fact, the number of individuals singing and teaching CCM is growing exponentially. With youth and enthusiasm on its side, it will be fascinating to see what the coming decades will bring. It is almost certain that CCM pedagogy will continue its ascent and influence in the pedagogic world.

Conclusion: Envisioning the Future

In May of 2018, I attended a symposium at the University of Southern California entitled "The Art and Science of Great Teaching: Celebrating the Legacy of William Vennard." The symposium celebrated not only Vennard's important contributions to voice pedagogy, but also acknowledged the inauguration of the Vennard Collection: a new archive of Vennard's personal writings, research files, and memorabilia. Keynote speakers at the symposium included Stephen F. Austin, Kenneth Bozeman, Thomas F. Cleveland, Cindy Dewey, Lynn Helding, Scott McCoy, and Kari Ragan.

While all of these speakers offered fascinating insights into twenty-first-century voice pedagogy, perhaps the most forward looking were the lectures by Helding and Ragan. Helding presented a session entitled "The Missing Mind: The Third Pillar of Voice Pedagogy." In it, she convincingly argued that singing voice research over the past several decades has focused overwhelmingly on biomechanics and acoustic theory, but the brain's role in singing—including topics such as cognition, perception, procedural learning, neuroplasticity, and motor learning theory—has been a largely neglected aspect of voice pedagogy.[18] Ragan proposed a dynamic new approach to the intersection of the interdisciplinary "voice team"—a term for the triumvirate core group consisting of the singing teacher, speech-language pathologist, and otolaryngologist— which she labels "Evidence-Based Voice Pedagogy." The interdisciplinary nature of our field has never been more front and center.

Looking at the history of voice pedagogy reveals a microcosm of the history of intellectual thought. The early Greek philosophers dabbled not only in philosophy, but also science, religion, mathematics, and a host of other topics. They were the great thinkers of the era, and all of these disciplines were young at the time. No mathematician studies "mathematics" (broadly) anymore—rather, they specialize. Polymaths like Vennard, Coffin, and Miller were pivotal figures who left an indelible mark during the earliest years of the fact-based era, but the twenty-first century suggests that a new paradigm is necessary.

The ever-expanding body of knowledge makes it increasingly impractical—if not impossible—for a singing teacher to be up-to-date in all arenas, making it all the more necessary to rely on a network of voice professionals who collectively represent various areas of expertise, including biomechanics, acoustic theory, psychology, and cognition, holistic practices, and all of the related health and wellness fields that are the province of medical professionals. The Big Bang of singing voice pedagogy continues to expand at exponential speed.

Notes

1. The Song of Deborah (Judges 5) and Miriam's Song of Triumph (Exodus 15:21) are two of the most significant psalm-like passages in the Tanakh/Old Testament.
2. I recommend this anthology as an ideal collection of "core readings" and as a basic introduction to topic of historical singing voice pedagogy.
3. Chiaroscuro, which means "light and shadow" in Italian, is a term that comes from visual art and painting. In voice pedagogy it refers to a classical tone quality that is balanced—neither too dark nor too bright. Appoggio—Italian for "support" or "lean"—refers to a breath management technique rooted in *bel canto* classical singing that advocates rib-based expansion and engagement of the thoracic-abdominal muscles during phonation.
4. Consult Stark's entire study for an in-depth exploration of the *bel canto* concept within the context of historical voice pedagogy.
5. These collective writings have recently been republished by Inside View Press under one cover as the title *Provenance: Historic Voice Pedagogy Viewed through a Contemporary Lens* (2017). Important predecessors to this column include series by Berton Coffin ("Vocal Pedagogy Classics," published from 1981–1984) and Craig Timberlake ("Practica Musicae," published from 1993–1997). Coffin's articles were collectively published in 1989 as *Historical Vocal Pedagogy Classics*.
6. *Coup de glotte* is a French term that translates as "stroke of the glottis." It was type of onset advocated by Manuel García II. The term is also controversial; pedagogues have long argued about the term's exact meaning and how the onset should be executed.
7. While there are many technique books available for purchase, most methodologies used in North American voice studios are in the public domain and can therefore be downloaded free of charge from such websites as imslp.org. Another collection entitled *Vocal Exercises: The Ultimate Collection* is available from CD Sheet Music, LLC.
8. Sell cites Galen (130–200) as the first laryngologist (2005, 190). If one accepts these two figures—Galen and García II—as pioneers, it is interesting that 1700 years elapsed before the invention of the laryngoscope.
9. NATS, which now uses this name, was founded in 1944.
10. This portion of the article is a crystalized version of a longer article published in a previous issue of the *Voice and Speech Review*. See "The Legacy of William Vennard and D. Ralph Appelman and Their Influence on Singing Voice Pedagogy: Reflections after 50 Years" (Hoch 2017).
11. I credit Scott McCoy for coining the term "fact-based." I first heard him use it in a lecture in 2007.
12. Miller is referring to *Vocal Wisdom: Maxims of Giovanni Battisa Lamperti*, translated by William Earl Brown.
13. Miller's other books include *Training Tenor Voices* (1993), *On the Art of Singing* (1996), *Singing Schumann* (1999), *Training Soprano Voices* (2000), *Solutions for Singers* (2004), and *Securing Baritone, Bass-Baritone, and Bass Voices* (2008).
14. Personal correspondence with Ingo Titze, June 14 2017.

15. Titze offered this explanation in person in as part of his "Principles of Voice Production" course at the Summer Vocology Institute (SVI) at the National Center for Voice and Speech (NCVS). The author enrolled in this class in June of 2013.
16. Much of the content in this section derives from the author's chapters previously published in his 2018 book, *So You Want to Sing Contemporary Commercial Music (CCM)* (Matthew 2018).
17. Riggs would soon settle in Los Angeles, where he established huge reputation as a teacher of famous singers in the recording industry. He also developed the Speech Level Singing (SLS)TM method.
18. The term "biomechanics," is used in this article to refer to the study of biological structures and function, not the method of actor training developed by Vsevolod Meyerhold (1874–1940).

Disclosure statement

No potential conflict of interest was reported by the author.

References

Bloem-Hubatka, Daniela. 2012. *The Old Italian School of Singing: A Theoretical and Practical Guide.* Jefferson, NC: McFarland and Company.

Bozeman, Kenneth W. 2013. *Practical Vocal Acoustics: Pedagogic Applications for Teachers and Singers.* Hillsdale, NY: Pendragon Press.

Bozeman, Kenneth W. 2017. *Kinesthetic Voice Pedagogy: Motivating Acoustic Efficiency.* Delaware, OH: Inside View Press.

Brown, William Earl. 1931. *Vocal Wisdom: Maxims of Giovanni Battista Lamperti.* Marlboro, NJ: Taplinger Publishing.

Coffin, Berton. [1976] 1987. *The Sounds of Singing: Vocal Techniques with Vowel-Pitch Charts.* Lanham, MD: Scarecrow Press.

Coffin, Berton. 1980. *Overtones of Bel Canto: Phonetic Basis of Artistic Singing with 100 Chromatic Vowel-Chart Exercises.* Lanham, MD: Scarecrow Press.

Coffin, Berton. 1989. *Historical Vocal Pedagogy Classics.* Lanham, MD: Scarecrow Press.

Doscher, Barbara. (1988) 1994. *The Functional Unity of the Singing Voice.* Lanham, MD: Scarecrow Press.

Günter, Horst. 1997. "Singing and Pedagogy from 1562–1854: What Do the Books Tell Us?" *Singing* 33.

Hoch, Matthew. 2014. *A Dictionary for the Modern Singer.* Lanham, MD: Rowman & Littlefield.

Hoch, Matthew. 2017. "The Legacy of William Vennard and D. Ralph Appelman and Their Influence on Singing Voice Pedagogy: Reflections after 50 Years." *Voice and Speech Review* 11 (3): 308–317.

Hoch, Matthew, ed. 2018. *So You Want to Sing Contemporary Commercial Music (CCM)*. Lanham, MD: Rowman & Littlefield.

Howell, Ian. 2016. "Parsing the Spectral Envelope: Toward a General Theory of Vocal Tone Color." DMA Dissertation, New England Conservatory.

LoVetri, Jennette, and Edrie Means Weekly. 2003. "Contemporary Commercial Music (CCM) Survey: Who's Teaching What in Non-Classical Music." *Journal of Voice* 17 (2): 207–215.

McCoy, Scott. [2004] 2012. *Your Voice: An Inside View*. Delaware, OH: Inside View Press.

Miller, Richard. [1977] 1997. *National Schools of Singing: English, French, German, and Italian Techniques of Singing Revisited*. Lanham, MD: Scarecrow Press.

Miller, Richard. 1986. *The Structure of Singing*. New York: Schirmer.

Miller, Richard. 2017. "Historical Overview of Voice Pedagogy." In *Vocal Health and Pedagogy: Science, Assessment, and Treatment*, edited by Robert Thayer Sataloff. San Diego: Plural Publishing.

Peterson, Gordon E., and Harold L Barney. 1952. "Control Methods Used in a Study of the Vowels." *Journal of the Acoustical Society of America* 24 (2): 175–184.

Sell, Karen. 2005. *The Disciplines of Vocal Pedagogy: Towards an Holistic Approach*. Burlington, VT: Ashgate.

Shigo, Daniel, and Dora Ohrenstein. 2006. "The New York Singing Teachers Association: A Brief History." *Voice Prints* 5 (5): 6–7.

Stark, James. 1999. *Bel Canto: A History of Vocal Pedagogy*. Toronto: University of Toronto Press.

Sundberg, Joan. 1977. "The Acoustics of the Singing Voice." *Scientific American* 236 (3): 82–91.

Sundberg, Johan. 1989. *The Science of the Singing Voice*. DeKalb, IL: Northern Illinois University Press.

Titze, Ingo. 1990. "Vocology." *The NATS Journal* 46 (3): 21.

Titze, Ingo. 1994. *Principles of Voice Production*. Upper Saddle River, NJ: Prentice Hall.

Titze, Ingo, and Katherine Verdolini Abbott. 2012. *Vocology: The Science and Practice of Voice Habilitation*. Salt Lake City: National Center for Voice and Speech.

Trimble, Michael. 2013. *Fundamentals of Great Vocal Technique: The Teachings of Michael Trimble*. Delaware, OH: Inside View Press.

Ware, Clifton. 1998. *Basics of Vocal Pedagogy: The Foundations and Process of Singing*. New York: McGraw-Hill.

Make the Door Open: Groundbreaking African American Teachers of Singing

Carl Du Pont

ABSTRACT

This article identifies some of the first African American professors of singing to integrate the faculties of notable music programs in the United States. The study examined archival sources on African American musicians, university records, and interviews conducted. Edna C. Williams, Thelma Waide Brown, Sylvia Olden Lee, Willis Patterson, Camilla Williams, Thomas Carey, and William Warfield were found to have made significant contributions as groundbreaking teachers, and their work is discussed. Significantly, a strong correlation exists between the timing of their appointments and the civil rights movement on college campuses at the University of Cincinnati, Indiana University, University of Michigan, and Oklahoma University. This suggests that political action played an influential role in encouraging music departments to include African American voice teachers on their faculties. The study suggests that their previous exclusion and subsequent admission to the academy after social action reinterprets higher music education as a racialized space. It simultaneously reappraises the historical significance of their careers as groundbreaking African American teachers of singing.

Introduction

The discussion of representation of African Americans, Latinos, Asians, the LGBTQ+ community, and people with disabilities on screens, in print, in boardrooms, and in elite classrooms has continued to gain relevance in recent years. Even as the American population continues to diversify, influence and access remain concentrated among the same population. In response to this mounting frustration communities with marginalized identities have activated and vocalized their displeasure. Vocal pedagogy experienced a similar moment during the Civil Rights Movement of the 1960s and 1970s, yet there has been regrettably little published about the history of Black teachers of singing who acted as pioneers to integrate the racialized spaces of the faculty ranks at Predominantly White Institutions (PWIs). These ethnographic accounts of PWIs are important because of the information they reveal about the difficult and rewarding work of creating inclusivity in higher music education.

Representation

Marian Anderson's momentous operatic debut at the Metropolitan Opera House on January 7, 1955 serves as a relevant starting point for a discussion of representation and blackness in classical singing. When she sang the role of Ulrica that night in Verdi's *Un Ballo in Maschera*, she became the first African American vocalist to perform on that stage (Story 1990, 36). However, as Leontyne Price eloquently said at a 75th birthday tribute to Ms. Anderson at Carnegie Hall:

> Whatever role she did that night, it wouldn't have mattered. Even if she had just walked on stage that night, the singular thing that she did was to make the door open. She did that, and I will be eternally indebted to her. (as quoted in Story 1990, 55)

The symbolism of the event had more importance than the notes Anderson sang, and that fact did not escape the house that night. Anderson's debut was as important for the Metropolitan Opera House, which had conveniently turned away black talent until then, as it was for the generation of singers who would be inspired by it.

As Price indicated in the above quote, African American opera singers discovered that simply opening their mouths to sing was a political statement at the time, regardless of the notes or the role. Racialized concepts of their body, and in turn their instruments, made their performance different in a way that drew attention to their skin as well as their sound (Eidsheim 2008, 40).

For African American teachers of singing, who matured artistically in this same atmosphere, teaching outside of the segregated Historically Black Colleges and Universities (HBCUs)[1] would have presented a similarly charged space. Their arrival on music faculties previously closed off to African Americans was a correlative struggle for recognition and acceptance that singers like Anderson strove for on the stage, albeit this one was outside of the spotlights. Even without having to address race issues in academia directly, the social awareness of the day implied that they were making a statement simply by being a Black presence in a White space.

This article, then, seeks to fill this gap in the vocal pedagogy literature. What follows is a historical overview of seminal early African American singing teachers, which includes their background and their legacy in the field. Each biographical entry is a crystallization of their life and impact. While some figures have more details than others, this discrepancy comes from the amount of historical research available. I conclude with a reflection on these legacies and music in higher education.[2]

Before the 1964 Civil Rights Act

Carole Brice (1918–1985) and Roland Hayes (1887–1976)

While HBCUs continued to remain favorable environments for Black artists to teach during and after their performing careers, Black Mountain College in North Carolina provided the first bridge to institutions that served mostly White students. This college was noted for the unique role it played in the avant-garde artistic scene in mid-twentieth century America, for some adventurous collaboration between Merce Cunningham and John Cage, as well as its enthusiasm for Arnold Schönberg. It was also in this artistic community, housed in a rural Southern town, that two African

American teachers of singing were appointed alongside other Black artists and scholars in 1945, only one year after the first Black students were admitted (Brody 2002, 241). Though recruited for month-long residencies rather than regular full-time appointments, the hiring of contralto Carol Brice and tenor Roland Hayes represented a concerted effort at integrating the music faculty by the director of the institute, musicologist Edward Lowinsky. He also ordered student ushers to inform visitors that the seating would not be segregated at Hayes's recital, which included European art songs, Spirituals, Creole, and Afro-Brazilian music (247).

Nevertheless, the Julius Rosenwald Foundation funded Brice and Hayes's participation through a grant. So, this was not a traditional teaching appointment; it was similar to an artist-in-residence arrangement (Harris 1987). That same foundation's director, William C. Haygood, compiled an article entitled "Negro Teachers in White Institutions" published in the 1946 issue of *The Phi Delta Kappan*; it listed all of the African Americans known to be teaching in PWIs. Of the 46 professors he identified during the 1945–1946 and 1946–1947 academic years, only 22 were on regular appointment. The 24 remaining instructors were part-time or visiting faculty like Brice and Hayes. As Haygood explained, this is still a cause for excitement since previously, in the 1930s, Black scholars could only expect invitations to lecture as a guest on Black culture or something similarly impermanent and Afrocentric. However, after 1940 and leading up to World War II, enrollment of Black students increased in tandem with the qualified Black men and women appointed to faculties (Haygood 1946). The door, it seems, had been unlocked.

Thelma Waide Brown (1896–1975)

Around the same time Haygood (1946) wrote the aforementioned article, Thelma Waide Brown began teaching at Chicago Musical College. Ms. Brown has the distinction of being the first African American voice teacher hired as a permanent faculty member by a PWI. The Chicago Musical College later joined with the music department at Roosevelt University in 1954, but it maintained the college's name and the personnel—including Brown as indicated on the Roosevelt website. An article written September 12 1957 in Chicago's daily newspaper for African American readers, *Daily Defender*, celebrated the soprano's tenth year on the faculty of Roosevelt University, therefore, giving her the distinction of being the only black vocal pedagogue hired on a permanent basis at a majority institution with a start date in the first half of the twentieth century.

Despite this achievement, Brown's historical record is restricted to the Thelma Waide Brown Collection that is a part of the digital archives at Roosevelt University. According to an obituary found there, several honorifics indicate that she was well-respected among her colleagues and also a very dedicated teacher. As early as 1954, she was chosen as the "Woman of the Year" by the Chicago chapter of the National Association of Business and Professional Women's Clubs. In 1961 and 1962 she received a Certificate of Award from the National Association of Negro Musicians (NANM) and the Chicago Music Association respectively. The Chicago Musical College honored her at a dinner in 1969 celebrating a 50-year career in singing and teaching; she was honored again by NANM for "Outstanding Achievements" in 1973.

After the 1964 Civil Rights Act

Edna C. Williams (1915–1994)

The 1964 Civil Rights Act and the executive order that followed linked federal funding to minority hires had a major impact on the educational system, yet these hires were mostly concentrated in the Midwest. The second Black voice teacher hired by a PWI was soprano Edna C. Williams in 1965 at Northern Illinois University; she remained on faculty until her retirement in 1994 at the rank of Professor of Music as reported in an article from *NIU Today*. Edna C. Williams' obituary stated that she received her Bachelor of Music and Master of Music degrees from the Chicago Musical College of Roosevelt University in 1957 and 1959, respectively, and she was a pupil of Harvey Ringwald. She won the John Hay Whitney Fellowship affording her the opportunity to study for 15 months in Vienna with Baron Hans Karg-Bebenburg and renowned accompanist, Professor Erik Werba. The significance of Thelma Waide Brown's and Edna C. Williams's academic posts lie in the unceremonious way they earned appointments as voice teachers through the traditional sequence of studying, performing, and teaching. This was a clear achievement considering the racial climate of the 1960s; however, it would be left up to the next group of pedagogues to open the door into highly ranked music programs that enjoyed the national spotlight.

The appointments of vocal coach Sylvia Olden Lee at the Cincinnati Conservatory of Music (CCM) in 1967, bass-baritone Willis Patterson at the University of Michigan (UM) in 1968, baritone Thomas Carey in 1969 at Oklahoma University (OU) and soprano Camilla Williams in 1977 at Indiana University (IU) were very different precisely because of the national visibility of these institutions. In that aspect, these figures represent the first appointments of African Americans at institutions that enjoyed influential national reputations in the 1960s and 1970s. The confluence of prestige and social activism on those respective campuses make these particularly interesting cases for claiming vocal pedagogy as a space for transformative inclusion.

The fact that music schools in the Midwest came before the private conservatories on the East Coast in hiring Black professors is perhaps not a coincidence. Although all work places were required as of 1961 to take "affirmative action" to ensure that their ranks were integrated, the slow rate of change left Black student groups unconvinced that their administrators truly cared about changing what they considered a "second-class citizenship" as noted in a *University of Cincinnati New Record* in May 18 1967 in the article "United Black Action Concerned with Campus Negro Condition." So, the students organized and held campus protests in a way only feasible on a large land-grant university campus setting. Both Lee and Patterson received the distinct impression that they were hired because the school had sought a Black candidate specifically to appease this unrest, and they attested to that fact. The institutions in the Midwest also had larger Black student populations with more solidarity from communal living than was possible in the comparatively small conservatories in big cities on the East Coast without student housing. Although their concern was with the academic environment as a whole, lasting effects were felt in the voice departments.

Sylvia Olden Lee (1917–2004)

Sylvia Olden Lee was considered by all accounts to be *the* preeminent scholar and authority on African American music during her lifetime, and she was equally sought after for coaching standard vocal repertoire (Lee and Nash 2001, 93). In 1994 Max Rudolf hired Lee to work with singers in the company's young artist program, making her the first Black member of the Metropolitan Opera staff (72).

Cincinnati Conservatory of Music

While working and living with her family in Europe, Lee received a call that would invite her once again to be a pioneer:

> Out of the blue in Sweden, I received an invitation to teach at the University of Cincinnati's College-Conservatory of Music in 1967. I wondered why they asked me because I'd had no contact with them. It took me six months to find out the reason for picking me. Someone had suggested that they must have one black on the faculty. (Lee and Nash 2001, 93)

Further investigation into the social climate on campus reveals that there was a groundswell of support for hiring Black faculty. In an article entitled "African American Heritage at UC" the *University of Cincinnati Magazine* noted that the University witnessed its most visible efforts at integration during the early 1960s driven by the efforts of the student organization, United Black Action (UBA). The UBA's main concern was changing the "second-class citizenship" of Black denizens on campus by making their collective voices heard (Rose 1967). The *University of Cincinnati News Record* shows how the University responded to those critical of their hiring efforts:

> Dick Baker, director of Community Relations spoke first, answering the Negro charge that UC employs only one full time black professor and one black campus policeman, and that there is a lack of Negro clerical help. Baker pointed out that the UC employs 418 Negros (sic), including six full time faculty members and four administration officials, and that six new professors will be added to the staff next year. (Kelly 1967, 4)

Although she is not mentioned by name, it is very likely that Sylvia Olden Lee is one of the six professors that had been invited to join the faculty. Her future employment was being used to deflect accusations of bias and prove that the administration was making earnest efforts at hiring Black professors.

In her memoir, Lee details the inhospitable environment she entered as CCM's first Black faculty member (Lee and Nash 2001, 73). She asked about arrival dates and accommodations in the same letter in which she accepted the offer, but received no response to her query. She informed the dean with the arrival time of her plane, but no one came to pick her up at the airport. Although the school had just built a brand-new music building, the dean told her that there was no studio for her. "I was walking around in that rainy season with nowhere to put my umbrella or books. I felt so homeless. We didn't have a place to live, and I didn't have anywhere to teach" (94). At the welcoming cocktail party for new faculty she was introduced to two other new music professors, both men from England. Not only were they met at the airport, but the school had also provided them with lodging. All three had traveled from Europe, but only two were treated as welcomed additions to the faculty.

The first year Lee spent at CCM ended with her being summoned to an ad hoc meeting by the board of trustees. Among the grievances lodged against her was the accusation that she did not allow the students to perform their operatic repertoire in Italian. Lee vehemently denied the accusations because she had been adamant in suggesting that music be performed in its original language instead of in English translation. This fact forced the new head of the opera department, Bob MacIntyre to recant and apologize. She later learned that the same Dean Watson (who hired her and showed such disregard to her travel from Sweden and accommodations in Cincinnati from the outset) had dictated the letter to MacIntyre. According to MacIntyre, he had been forced to make the accusation with the threat of losing his job (Lee and Nash 2001, 98)

Obviously, Lee was unhappy in that environment, but did not have to stay so for long. Max Rudolf had just been hired as head of the Opera Department at the Curtis Institute in Philadelphia (Lee and Nash 2001, 100). He invited her to join his team at Curtis, having already worked with Lee at the Metropolitan Opera. As she so simply stated, "In 1970 I was the first black hired at the Curtis Institute." Helene van Rossum, the archivist at the Curtis Institute of Music, confirmed in an email to the author that she remained on faculty until 1990, a 20-year tenure.

The Teacher

Kevin Short, Associate Professor at the University of Maryland, was introduced to Sylvia Olden Lee while a student at the Curtis Institute of Music and was interviewed for this project about his history with Lee (Du Pont 2014). As a coach, Short observed that Lee's style was consistent whether coaching Schubert lieder or Spirituals. She insisted on prompting, finding the motivation behind each individual phrase, and linking each successive idea to the next in a chain. When asked how the students responded to this type of approach, Short responded that the students loved her, as long as they did their homework. She believed singers should wake up very early and study their music every day. Lee preferred commitment and hard work to beautiful voices disconnected from the meaning of the text. As such, Short felt her genius was best revealed in stripping away artifice and getting to the core of an aria or song.

Sylvia Olden Lee's most enduring legacy was the amount of formidable collaborations with many of the world's leading African American singers. This includes Kathleen Battle, Jessye Norman, Paul Robeson, Lawrence Winters, Osceola Davis, Martina Arroyo, and Simon Estes.

Willis Patterson (1930-)

Willis Patterson began his teaching career at Southern University in Louisiana. He then moved to Virginia State College, all the while still concertizing actively as a recitalist and opera singer. Interviewed by the author at the National Association of Negro Musicians in Nashville, Tennessee in 2013, Patterson admitted being surprised when the University of Michigan first contacted him about a possible opening. He had just been recently tenured at Virginia State College, when voice faculty chairman, John McCollum, asked him if he would be interested in applying for the job in a letter dated September 22, 1967. Patterson was exactly what the school was searching for, being that he was an Ann Arbor Native, a former Fulbright fellow, and had earned his bachelor's, master's, and doctorate degrees all there at the University of Michigan. Patterson fit the school's profile, but the University of Michigan no longer fit his needs. His singing career was based mostly on the East Coast and included touring HBCUs in the South; Virginia was much closer to New York City and the southern states than Ann Arbor. In addition, Patterson was very happy with the musical community at Virginia State College, and his family's fondness for the Petersburg, Virginia area made him understandably apprehensive about uprooting them and moving to Michigan. Nevertheless, the appeal of the University of Michigan and an agreement to allow Patterson to transfer his rank to Ann Arbor tipped the scales.

When Dr. Patterson joined the University of Michigan, he was not just the first Black voice teacher on faculty, but he was the first Black professor in the School of Music. Patterson identified that Black students had begun applying pressure to the administration in the form of student uprisings on Michigan's campus to achieve more representation in the student and faculty bodies. He indicated that while there was no explicit acknowledgement linking his hiring as a direct response to these student lead actions, the dissatisfaction was already palpable and the time for University of Michigan to make concerted efforts to integrate had come (Patterson 2015).

Black Action Movement

In 1962, University of Michigan was advised to take steps to increase integration at the student and faculty level because a federal investigation found a substantial amount of racial bias in their hiring process as detailed in "Open It Up or Shut It Down: The 1970 Black Action Movement Strike at Michigan" for *The Ann Arbor Chronicle*. As a result, a committee appointed by University of Michigan president, Harlan Hatcher, established The Opportunity Awards Program, but this program only managed to increase Black enrollment from 2% to 3% between 1964 and 1969. Black students, unhappy with this rate of progress began flexing their political muscle with a sit-in at the University of Michigan administration building in 1968 following the assassination of Dr. Martin Luther King. One year later, Black student groups were still unimpressed with the University's efforts and coalesced to form the Black Action Movement (BAM), deciding it was time to be even more proactive. On February 5 1970, they initiated demonstrations that eventually led to the 18-day shutdown of University of Michigan's Ann Arbor campus and garnered considerable media attention. BAM's stated goals were an increase in Black enrollment and Black faculty to 10% by the 1973–1974 school year (Blonston 1970).

John McCollum's explorative letter to Willis Patterson arrived before student discontent erupted on the Ann Arbor campus, but after the federal investigation officially recognized that the hiring and admission processes at the university had maintained an academic culture out of touch with the educational needs of the larger community. Student dissatisfaction with the rate of minority representation on faculty would reach its zenith more than a year after Patterson began at the University of Michigan, signifying that African Americans there wanted even more than the administration's mere acquiescence to hire Blacks. They wanted more African Americans who would make significant contributions to the institutionalization of Black culture in order to transform what felt like a tolerant environment to an affirming one. Willis Patterson proved to be an ideal addition to the faculty precisely for that reason.

Positive—But Mixed

As the first African American teacher on faculty in the University of Michigan's Department of Music, Patterson felt the environment was "By and large [...] positive —but mixed" (Du Pont 2014, 63). His presence was a dynamic change to the face of the voice faculty, and he was aware of this, especially as a former student of the university now elevated to the level of his former teachers. The only incident of true tension that Patterson expressed when interviewed occurred when he took over the reins of the Glee Club, becoming its first African American conductor. The Glee Club, according to Patterson, had the habit of functioning as a de facto White fraternity, and it had its own structure of self-governance to which the men adhered. Patterson's insistence on being the ultimate authority in the group caused, in his words, "quite a bit of friction," for the first six years of his tenure (64). He ultimately overcame this challenge and won the affection of the group and an invitation to their reunions.

Anthology of Art Songs by Black American Composers

Willis Patterson (1977) compiled and published the *Anthology of Art Songs by Black American Composers*. As voice teachers often do, he surveyed the available collections of American art songs to find assignments for his students. After thumbing through eight different collections representing 139 compositions and over 80 different composers, he felt a significant group of composers had been mostly overlooked. Only four of the composers in those eight anthologies were Black. Patterson's solution, much in keeping with the Black Nationalist sentiment sweeping the nation, was to create something that celebrated exactly those characteristics that song publishers had conveniently ignored. His compilation was not the first of its kind, but it was the first to be deemed indispensable, according to a review written in 1980 by Harvard University (Wright 1980). Writing for the *Black Music Research Journal* Donald Ivey (1981) commented, "When a collection as important as the *Anthology of Art Songs by Black American Composers* comes along, it should stir more than the usual amount of interest among musicians of all varieties, not only vocalists and vocal pedagogues." Patterson's anthology had not only given America's Black songwriters a discernable group identity, but it also rendered this music accessible for analyzing, teaching, and performing in both academic and professional concert venues.

Writing for the *New York Times* over 20 years later in "The Black Art Song: A Forgotten Repertory" Cori Ellison describes Patterson's 1977 publication as groundbreaking for assuming the herculean task of bringing Black art songs out of the shadow of Spirituals, blues, and jazz music. Patterson (1996) would go on to write an essay for the *Black Music Research Journal* entitled "The African American Art Song: A Musical Means for Special Teaching and Learning," in which he eloquently asserts the necessity of Black voices and Black art songs to the cannon. The article ends with a particularly moving tribute to these songs to which Patterson dedicated himself so wholeheartedly:

> The art song is indeed, not antithetical to the African American experience. To the contrary, the art song represents a marvelous and unique opportunity to teach and preserve some of the very best and most noble aspects of American musical and cultural history. For those who will avail themselves of their wisdom, African American art songs are musically beautiful and vocally challenging. They bestow cultural enrichment and empowerment upon performers and audiences alike. (Patterson 1996, 310)

The Teacher

Patterson was eventually named Associate Dean of the University of Michigan School of Music, and he served in that capacity for 20 years according to an interview by White and Thompkins (2012) preserved in the African American Cultural and Historical Museum of Oral History. He attributed his success as a voice trainer to his time spent at HBCUs because there he had to do "everything in the field or in the area and discipline of vocal music—choral conducting, directing operas, training voice, [and] teaching pedagogy" (Du Pont 2014, 69). He also became very involved with recruiting minority students and faculty to the University of Michigan by his continual contact with HBCUs through concertizing and his connections to other singing teachers in the field. He helped train Jessye Norman while she was a student at the University of Michigan, and he recruited internationally renowned African American singers George Shirley and Shirley Verrett to join the faculty.

Thomas Carey (1932–2002)

Thomas Carey began appearing at Oklahoma University (OU) in 1968 as an Artist-in-Residence and was promoted to Visiting Professor in 1969, as noted in a *Tulsa World* article on January 25 2002. Eventually he would receive the Governor's Artist of the year award in 1975 and the Oklahoma Man of the Year Award in 1976. He was honored with the OU Distinguished service award in 1985 and appointed as OU Regents Professor in 1994.

His arrival, however, came at a tenuous time. Oklahoma University began dealing with the issue of integration in a very public way in 1948. George McLaurin, a 70-year-old Black school teacher, applied to the doctoral program at the university's School of Education. He was admitted but forced to sit in his own row, and sometimes his own room during lectures. McLaurin appealed the school's treatment of him to the Supreme Court, which decided in *McLaurin V. Oklahoma* that this type of segregation denied the plaintiff the intangible benefits of discussions that would prepare him to be a leader in society (Gates 2011, 322).

Not surprisingly, 20 years later the atmosphere on campus was still tense; George Henderson's (2010) account, *Race and the University: A Memoir*, vividly describes the environment that he entered as a newly hired Black professor of sociology at Oklahoma University in the 1960s. Most property owners would not rent to Blacks, and Henderson discovered that Norman property owners would not sell to a Black family either, after his family's first, second, and third choice of homes were taken off the market once they expressed interest (10). Many of the students felt the same sense of unwelcome on the college campus:

> Shortly after I began teaching in August 1967, a group of Black students asked me what I was going to do about "our situation." They rattled off some shocking data regarding the Norman campus: relatively few Black students were enrolled at the University. There were no Black administrators or coaches, and only ten or so Blacks were employed there, as extension specialists and in lesser staff positions. (Henderson 2010, 26)

The value Black students placed on having representation on the faculty was made explicit when the university's Afro-American Student Union drafted the *Black*

Declaration of Independence and presented it to President J. Herbert Hollomon on March 4 1969. The preamble stated that little progress had been made that did away with the University's "institutionalized racism inherent in its creation, government, and administration," and cited the president's "treachery and deceit" in his claim that there was not enough money to attract Black professors to campus (Henderson 2010, 106).

When Carey arrived, he was in the middle of a flourishing performing career, so initially his time in Norman was limited, but he made a significant impact. According to Henderson's memoir (2010), Carey and his wife, contralto Carol Brice who was hired a few years later, brought the number of black faculty from three to five and increased the number of black-owned homes in the town from 1 to 2 (116).

OU's President J. Herbert Hollomon expressed gratitude to Carey in a letter dated July 1, 1970, for the support he showed in the president's efforts toward increasing tolerance and sensitivity on the Norman campus; this demonstrated that although Carey was hired as a voice teacher, his contribution to improving the campus went beyond OU's Music Department. As a professor, he helped change the face of the student body by effectively recruiting and training Black singers. Even as late as 1998, four years after retiring at the rank of Distinguished Regents Professor of Music, Carey was still in communication with the Equal Opportunity and Affirmative Action Office of The University of Oklahoma. In a letter addressed to Jerry E. Jensen on July 13, 1998, he described his concern about OU's commitment to a multiracial university community in the School of Music's faculty search process.

Carey also sought to extend his influence outside of the school as well. In 1971 he joined the newly formed Norman Human Rights Commission. This commission was purposed and authorized to handle the complaints of discriminatory practices in housing, public accommodations, and employment. Together with wife Carol Brice, Carey co-founded the Cimarron Circuit Opera Company in 1975. Apparently, the two noticed a dearth of performing outlets for their students, and Carey established this opera company in order to give more stage opportunities to aspiring singers (Henderson 2010, 224). In order to raise money for the Cimarron Circuit Opera Company, he co-produced a jazz concert in 1984 that attracted 300 people and the interest of the Norman Arts and Humanities Council. With the support of that council, Carey's brainchild blossomed into an annual event called "Jazz in June" that has become a staple on the city's calendar.[3]

The *Tulsa World* article stated that the president of Oklahoma University, who knew Carey for over 30 years, appreciated that Carey invested in his students and that his teaching came at the expense of what could have been a formidable performing career. On Carey's impact at OU, the president stated, "He leaves a great legacy through the lives of all of those students who have known him," as noted in *Tulsa World*.

William Warfield (1920–2002)

The gains made by these pioneers in the 1960s continued to reverberate through the music conservatories in the following decade. Bass William Warfield would join the faculty at the University of Illinois Champaign-Urbana in 1976 as he described in his autobiography *William Warfield: My Life and My Music* (Miller and Warfield 1991). He relays how he believed himself to be much more approachable than the average professor; students, especially black students who had never been so far away from home, found a new home at his house where socializing and home-cooked meals were the norm. He even counted the first African American vocalists to receive their doctorates from the University of Illinois as his pupils.

Camilla Williams (1919–2012)

Camilla Williams was the first African American professor of voice at Indiana University (IU) when she joined in 1977. She also became the first African American professor to teach at Beijing's Central Conservatory when she was a guest there in 1983, according to the Jacob's School of Music internal blog "The Jacobs School of Music Mourns the Passing of Opera Star Camilla Williams." By the time she retired in 1997 from IU, she had become a beloved faculty member known for her furs, her wit, and her charm. She received one of the highest honors the university president could bestow when in 2009 she was the recipient of the Indiana University President's Medal for Excellence. In 2010, she was awarded the Sagamore of the Wabash, the highest honor the Governor of Indiana can bestow, for bringing distinction and honor to the state.

Before Camilla Williams came to the IU Bloomington campus as the first African American teacher of voice, race-relations were already part of the consciousness of students and administrators. The assassination of Martin Luther King, Jr. in 1968 encouraged the members of Indiana University's Afro-Afro-American Student Association (AAASA) to become increasingly vocal about the limited number of African Americans at the administrative, faculty, and student levels of the university, as detailed in the Indiana University Student Archive Exhibit called "The 1968 Little 500 Sit-in." Their first order of business was an open letter to the president of the university, Elvis Jacob Stahr, demanding more concrete measures be put into place for the hiring of Black faculty and the admission of Black students. President Stahr's response came in a speech he delivered at the National Conference of Negroes in Higher Education shortly after AAASA's letter was publicized. Stahr stated that he believed White universities should avoid hiring Black faculty from Black institutions because they were an important part of those colleges and universities. He also informed the group that he did not want to actively recruit more Black students until the university developed "effective methods of instruction, geared to meet the special need they may have—so that they are likely to succeed, not fail, when they do enroll" (Wynkoop 2002, 122).

His argument can be explained by the fact that Black students at Indiana University were much more likely than White students to drop out of school; almost half of those students left without graduating. Although Black students in the 1960s found IU Bloomington to be among the more racially tolerant of the Midwest's college campuses and even though IU was the first major American university to approve a Black studies program, the small numbers of Black representation left members feeling vulnerable. African Americans made up approximately 6% of Indiana's population in the 1960s, yet they were only 2% of the student body. There were less than 10 Black faculty members, and no Black administrators on the entire campus. President Stahr's predecessor, Herman B. Wells, was held in high regard for his progressive policies in regard to students of color, but the strong influence of the Ku Klux Klan in Indiana state politics and the Southern cultural roots of south-central Indiana made Indiana University a challenging environment for the Black students and faculty members alike (Wynkoop 2002).

When Camilla Williams joined the faculty of Indiana University in 1977 as the first Black voice teacher, she added another accomplishment to the list of firsts in her career (Williams and Shonekan 2011, 201).Williams debuted as Madama Butterfly with the New York City Opera in 1946, and by doing so she earned a place in history as the first African American female opera singer to appear with a major American opera company. In the 1960s, Williams frequently served as a cultural ambassador for the State Department touring throughout Africa, Asia, and Israel. She also sang at the 1963 March on Washington right before Martin Luther King, Jr. gave his historic "I Have a Dream" speech, when Marian Anderson got stuck in traffic, as reported by Jacobs School of Music at her passing.

Williams was teaching at Queens College in New York City in 1975, when she began to receive phone calls from Charles Webb, Dean of the IU School of Music, and Hermann Hudson, Professor and Chair of the African American studies at IU. Margaret Harshaw had recommended Williams, and they wanted her to become the first Black professor of voice (Williams and Shonekan 2011). Dean Webb and Professor Hudson enlisted Undine Smith Moore and Michael Gordon, a young Black professor in the music education division who happened to also be a fellow alumnus of Williams's alma mater, Virginia State College. They orchestrated a two-year campaign to convince Williams to move to Bloomington. Yet, it still took some convincing of the divine order for her to accept the position. During her visit, the choir at the First United Methodist Church sang her mother's favorite hymn "What a Friend We Have in Jesus."

Williams felt that the move to Indiana was the best move she ever made, but it was still a difficult one. Returning to campus after lunch with her colleagues, Williams noted a very handsome condominium apartment complex, and said, "I would love to live there." To which another professor in the car responded, "You can't live there, Camilla" (Williams and Shonekan 2011, 201). It was then made clear to Williams that her professional success could not completely insulate her from the borderlines still drawn because of her skin color. She wrote, "Shaking my head silently, I looked away across the road at the not-so-impressive apartments opposite Woodcrest. I swiped at the stubborn and familiar tears that threatened the corners of my eyes and we rode back to school in a stony sad silence" (203).

Professor William's teaching philosophy was based on her love of teaching the technical aspects of singing (Nash 2002). She focused on how to place the voice and how to develop good diction. She also felt that her teaching, musicianship, and singing all benefitted from the concert and chamber music that had become a mainstay of her career:

> I had high expectations of all my students and did not compromise standards. They had to
> work hard and listen to my instructions. I did not just care about their vocal performance,
> but also the quality of their lives and their self-esteem. (Williams and Shonekan 2011, 219)

Williams became a particular favorite of Dean Charles Webb, who described her as "bigger than life" in an interview at his home in Bloomington (Du Pont 2014). The two often performed in recitals together as a duo, and their last performance was in the

White House at the invitation of President Bill Clinton. Webb described Williams as both a pacesetter and a pioneer, because of her accomplishments on the stage and on Indiana's faculty. He was also convinced that her presence as an "advertised commodity" drew Black talent to the school's voice department, some of which sought her out as a voice teacher, while others simply appreciated the presence of an African American on faculty and studied with other teachers. For Dean Webb, her impact was unmistakable:

> I have called her a role model, a mentor for young musicians, and her contributions to the world of music are really history now. She will be remembered as a beautiful, courageous, giving and loving person by generations long into the future. (Jacobs School of Music 2012, 1)

Reflection and Implications

This article is ongoing historical research, and it has clear implications for understanding music in higher education: its past, present, and future. We must recognize that our institutions did not have a colorblind history. *The Agony of Education: Black Students at White Colleges and Universities* states:

> The desegregation of college and university faculties has come slowly in the United States. [...] On and off college campuses, a majority of white Americans share a heritage permeated by racialized thinking. Much of this racial thought is conscious, but some is half-conscious or even subconscious. (Feagin, Vera, and Imani 1996, 69)

That conscious, half-conscious, and subconscious racialized thinking presented a real barrier that these groundbreaking teachers encountered in their journeys. As talented, prepared, and pedigreed as the pedagogues outlined in this article were, they were sought and hired as part of a concerted effort between the student body and the administration to make diverse representation an important factor of uprooting the status quo. The implications of this would likely have exacted a psychic toll on all of them. In his autobiography, *The Unlikely Saga of a Singer from Ann Arbor*, Patterson (2015) wrote:

> I felt no sense of insecurity or lack of competence in comparison to my new colleagues at the U. of M. I sensed only my potential inability to overcome their possible self-perceptions of social and professional superiority with a certain calmness and grace. I knew myself to be under an intense—even if unintended and unknown to themselves —scrutiny by my new colleagues. (210)

Presently, although diversity and inclusion have emerged as buzzwords for many organizations including conservatories, the efforts made so far have resulted only in incremental gains. A 2016–2017 data summary compiled by the Higher Education Arts and Data Services and commissioned by the National Association of Schools of Music bulletin demonstrates that a truly diverse conservatory remains elusive. Of the 621 institutions reporting, Black/African American faculty make up 4.7%, American Indian/Alaska Natives 0.4%, Asian 4.9%, Hispanic 3.7%, Native Hawaiian/Pacific Islander 0.5%, White 84.3%, and other 1.6% (Higher Education Arts Data Services 2017). Complacency with this modest improvement on the faculty level hints to a cynical view of the potential positive impact that a truly representative faculty could have on higher music education as a whole.

In the future, collecting qualitative data about the student and faculty experiences of underrepresented groups in schools of music could shed light on the reason that these numbers do not show a growth in diversity. Additional attention could also be given to the issue of representative leadership in higher education. The highest levels of arts administration in the collegiate and on the professional level have maintained a lack of diversity despite the nation's changing demographics, and the changing needs of the arts organizations. Rodney Miller (1993) asserts in his book *Institutionalizing Music: The Administration of Music Programs in Higher Education* "The average music chair is a 50-year-old male tenured professor" (54). Although the other does not address ethnicity in his assessment, whiteness is implied as the default, and this reality is observable. The decisions made on hiring are taking place at this level.

Long-Term Effects

In reflecting on the historical ideas in this article, I assert that the contributions of the first African American singing teachers who worked at prestigious Predominantly White Institutions in the 1960s and 1970s had a long-term effect. By engaging in a space previously reserved for White Americans or Europeans at a time of racial struggle and turmoil in the United States, their teaching experience was complicated by notions of their readiness and competence ingrained in students and colleagues by systematic racism. Despite that climate, their visibility, as they excelled as members of highly regarded vocal departments, affirmed the ability of African Americans to be full participants at high levels of competition and responsibility within the musical establishment. This same visibility also brought a new awareness to students of every hue, seeing African Americans endowed with and executing positions of authority within the conservatory system. In essence, they were able to make a dynamic shift in the perception and reception of the African Americans who would follow in their footsteps.

Institutionalized racism was so systematic in the United States that the fight for racial uplift had to be waged on every available front; vocal pedagogy was no exception. Even in the absence of a conspiracy to prevent African Americans from joining the professoriate, there was an effective system that managed to exclude teachers of color. This was evident, despite African American participation in art music for many years as students in conservatories and performers on stage.

The groundbreaking pioneers profiled here shattered the lingering cognitive barrier to African American participation on the voice faculties of America's premiere conservatories and schools of music. They were aided by the Civil Rights Movement in the national agenda, Black student organizations' demands for greater faculty representation, and the implementation of statutes that forced federally funded entities to take proactive steps to hire Black talent. They were prepared through excellent training in the United States and Europe, successful international concert and operatic careers, and in some cases teaching experience gained from employment at HBCUs. Once they had assumed duties at artistically demanding institutions, they fulfilled their jobs expertly and were rewarded with long tenures and increasingly higher ranks. They made the door open.[4]

Notes

1. Historically Black Colleges and Universities (HBCUs) are higher education institutions in the United States. These schools were founded before the Civil Rights Act of 1964 and historically and primarily served the African American community. Generally, they were founded because segregation laws in the United States (predominately in the American south) prevented African Americans from acceptance into other institutions of higher learning.
2. This article is a crystalized version of my dissertation, "Pioneering African American Teachers of Singing" (Du Pont 2014).
3. See the event's website at http://jazzinjune.org/.
4. For a list of African American teachers of singing referenced in this article and other teachers discussed in the dissertation this study is based on (Du Pont 2014), see Appendix, online supplemental materials.

Disclosure statement

No potential conflict of interest was reported by the author.

References

Blonston, Gary. 1970. "Black-White Unity Boosts U.M. Boycott."*Detroit Free Press*, March 29.
Brody, Martin. 2002. "The Scheme of the Whole: Black Mountain and the Course of American Modern Music." In *Black Mountain College: Experiment in Art*, edited by Vincent Katz, 225–251. Cambridge, MA: MIT Press.
Eidsheim, Nina Sun. 2008. "Voice as a Technology of Selfhood: Towards an Analysis of Racialized Timbre and Vocal Performance." PhD diss., University of California.
Feagin, Joe R., Hernán Vera, and Nikitah Imani. 1996. *The Agony of Education: Black Students at White Colleges and Universities*. New York: Routledge.
Gates, Henry Louis. 2011. *Life upon These Shores: Looking at African American History,1513-2008*. New York: Alfred A. Knopf.
Harris, Mary Emma. 1987. *The Arts at Black Mountain College*. Cambridge, MA: MIT Press.
Haygood, William C. 1946. "Negro Teachers in White Institutions." *The Phi Delta Kappan* 28 (2): 74–75.
Henderson, George. 2010. *Race and the University: A Memoir*. Norman, OK: University of Oklahoma Press.
Higher Education Arts Data Services. 2017. "Music Data Summaries 2016-2017." https://secure3.vaultconsulting.com/HEADS/.

Ivey, Donald. 1981. "Willis Patterson's *Anthology of Art Song by Black American Composers*." *Black Music Research Journal* 2: 106–126. doi:10.2307/779414.

Jacobs School of Music. 2012. "Remembering Camilla Williams: 1919-2012" Accessed 1 May 2014. https://blogs.music.indiana.edu/camillawilliams/.

Kelly, Mike. 1967. "Committee Answers Negro Bias Charges." *University of Cincinnati New Record*, May 11.

Lee, Sylvia Olden, and Elizabeth Nash. 2001. *The Memoirs of Sylvia Olden Lee, Premier African American Classical Vocal Coach*. Lewiston, NY: Edwin Mellen Press.

Miller, Alton, and William Warfield. 1991. *My Music and My Life*. Champaign, IL: Sagamore Publishing.

Miller, Rodney E. 1993. *Institutionalizing Music: The Administration of Music Programs in Higher Education*. Springfield, IL: Charles C. Thomas Publisher.

Nash, Elizabeth. 2002. "A Day with Camilla Williams." *The Opera Quarterly* 18 (2): 225–230. doi:10.1093/oq/18.2.219.

Patterson, Willis. 1977. *Anthology of Art Songs by Black American Composers*. New York: Edward B. Marks Music Company.

Patterson, Willis. 1996. "The African American Art Song: A Musical Means for Special Teaching and Learning." *Black Music Research Journal* 16 (2): 303–310. doi:10.2307/779333.

Patterson, Willis. 2015. *The Unlikely Saga of a Singer from Ann Arbor: The Autobiography of Willis C. Patterson, Basso*. Ann Arbor: Maize Books.

Du Pont, Carl F., Jr. 2014. "Pioneering African American Teachers of Singing." DMA diss., University of Miami.

Rose, Bryan. 1967. "United Black Action Concerned with Campus Negro Condition." *University of Cincinnati New Record*, May 18.

Story, Rosalyn M. 1990. *And so I Sing: African American Divas of Opera and Concert*. New York: Warner Books.

White, Laurie, and Rolando Thompkins. 2012. *Interview of William Patterson*. Ann Arbor, MA: African American Cultural and Historical Museum Oral History. Accessed 23 June 2014. http://www.aadl.org/aachmvideos/willis_patterson.

Williams, Camilla, and Stephanie Shonekan. 2011. *The Life of Camilla Williams: African American Classical Singer and Opera Diva*. Lewiston, NY: Edwin Mellen Press.

Wright, Josephine. 1980. "Anthology of Art Song by Black American Composers, for Voice and Piano by Willis Patterson." *Notes* 37 (2): 423–424. doi:10.2307/939537.

Wynkoop, Mary Ann. 2002. *Dissent in the Heartland: The Sixties at Indiana University*. Bloomington, IN: Indiana University Press.

A Historian's Journey with Sylvia Olden Lee and Camilla Williams, African American Opera Pioneers

Elizabeth Nash

ABSTRACT

This article is a historiography that explores and reflects upon the author's study of Sylvia Olden Lee and Camilla Williams, African American women who were each a pioneer in operatic performance. The article highlights Lee and Williams's contributions to singing performance and pedagogy, and while doing so, the author reflects on her personal journey as a historian and biographer of African American vocal history.

This article is a historiography and a reflection on my work as a historian and biographer of Sylvia Olden Lee and Camilla Williams. Each woman had a profound influence on my life as a performer, teacher, and scholar. This following article chronicles my journey with these trailblazing African American opera singers and discusses their legacy.

At the time of Marian Anderson's death on April 8, 1993, I asked my voice class if they had read the obituary tribute to the distinguished African American contralto in *The New York Times* (Kozinn 1993). None of them had even heard of her. I immediately contacted my African American reference librarian colleague and friend, Professor Patricia Turner. She was a discography expert on the recordings of African American classical singers and had collected hundreds of rare recordings, including nineteenth-century wax cylinders of the Fiske University Jubilee Singers. I asked her if she would tell my class about Miss Anderson and play some of her recordings. She did and included selections by Antoinette Garnes, Florence Cole Talbot, Roland Hayes, Todd Duncan, Camilla Williams, Dorothy Maynor, and Paul Robeson. I was unfamiliar with most of these singers and was astounded by their beautiful voices and masterful vocal techniques. Roland Hayes reminded me of the great Irish tenor John McCormack, and Dorothy Maynor's singing of "Depuis le jour" was the finest rendition of that aria from Charpentier's opera *Louise* I had ever heard.

After class, I told Patricia that she should be teaching a seminar on these singers. "I love their voices," she replied,

> but I cannot analyze them technically the way you did in class. How about we both teach a seminar together. I'll lecture on their lives and on the Spiritual, while you discuss their vocal techniques and styles of interpreting the classical repertoire.[1]

This resulted in our team teaching the seminar, African American Singers: The Classical Tradition, for the Afro-American Studies Department. One young woman came up after the session on the Original Fiske Jubilee Singers who had performed for Queen Victoria. Patricia had shown a slide of the famous painting in Jubilee Hall at Fiske University of the elegantly attired singers in the presence of the Queen. "I never knew that our ancestors dressed like that in those days!" This led us to decide on writing a book chronicling the history of all these singers from the 1850s to the present. We began collecting printed material and decided to request interviews with two distinguished African American classical musical pioneers: Sylvia Olden Lee and Camilla Williams.

Mrs. Lee had been my vocal coach when I was an opera singer in Germany. I often wondered what had become of her. One evening while watching a PBS program on Kathleen Battle and Wynton Marsalis's video of the *Baroque Duets*, she appeared in a coaching session with Ms. Battle. I wrote Mrs. Lee a letter care of Kathleen Battle and received a phone call from her asking, "Where have you been all these years"? She was living in Philadelphia busily coaching and accompanying at Howard University in Washington D.C. I learned that Patricia knew Mrs. Lee as well from attending her master classes at the annual conferences of the National Association of Negro Musicians.

Patricia and I were going to interview Todd Duncan at his home in Washington, D.C. Mr. Duncan had created the role of Porgy in the 1936 Broadway premiere of George Gershwin's *Porgy and Bess*. Patricia contacted Mrs. Lee and asked if we could also interview her at Howard University to learn of her professional work with African American classical singers. She readily agreed. When we met with Mrs. Lee, we discovered that both she and her ancestors were a part of American musical history. Realizing that her life story should be preserved, I suggested she write her memoirs. At first, she refused until I offered to co-author them with her. This was followed by fifty hours of taped interviews in my Minneapolis home. Not only did she relate her life story, but she discussed her fascinating teaching methodology in both the book and appendices (Nash 2001. The book is a combination memoir and teaching tool. I learned that Mrs. Lee was the world's leading authority on the Spiritual and had composed numerous arrangements, many of which were performed by Jessye Norman and Kathleen Battle in their concerts. Also, she was the first African American hired onto the musical staffs of both the Metropolitan Opera and the Curtis Institute of Music.

Serving as scribe to this country's first world renowned African American classical vocal interpretation coach included marvelous perquisites. In July 1996, Mrs. Lee was invited to join Phyllis Curtin, Sarah Caldwell, and Jon Vickers as honored guests at the Tanglewood Music Center for the fiftieth anniversary gala performance of the American premiere of Benjamin Britten's opera *Peter Grimes*. I had the privilege of accompanying her that evening at the performance and will long remember listening to the animated conversation of these four distinguished musical figures who were associated with this opera either in 1946 or later.

On June 29, 1997, I attended Opera North's celebration of Mrs. Lee's 80th birthday and her contributions to the world of music for over 60 years. It was a fitting tribute given that she as the former musical director at Opera North. The Honorary Co-Chairs were Jessye Norman, Kathleen Battle, and Mayor Edward Rendell. Philadelphia's Congregation Rodeph Shalom synagogue was filled with family, colleagues, students, and friends. Some of them were from Mrs. Lee's early days at Howard University and the Oberlin Conservatory. Moving written tributes came from Jessye Norman, Kathleen Battle, Maya Angelou, Mayor Edward Rendell, and Governor Tom Ridge. "Who is Sylvia, What is She?" wrote Jessye Norman.

"The most energetic, musical and dedicated muse one could ever imagine" (as quoted in Opera North 1997, 28). "Thank you for all you give to the music world," added Kathleen Battle (as quoted in Opera North, 18). And Maya Angelou stated:

> Great monuments, great ideas and some great women were revealed to us four score years ago. In 1917 the world prepared to erase hate, racism, and violence from the planet. Of course, that was called World War I. Had the great powers known that in the same year Sylvia Olden Lee was going to be born we could have avoided World War I and waited for the beauty, intelligence, dedication and talent of Sylvia Olden who would be given to us. She was sent to bring us music, great harmonies, laughter, art, beauty and love. I join countless who are grateful that she came and came to stay this long. (as quoted in Opera North 1997, 22)

There were musical performances, including Mattiwilda Dobbs' limpid "O mio babbino caro" (Giacomo Puccini's *Gianni Schicchi*), George Shirley's impassioned "Lit'l Boy," and William Warfield's rousing "Ol' Man River" (Jerome Kern's *Show Boat*). "I would only come out of retirement to sing for Sylvia Olden Lee," said Miss Dobbs, whose words expressed the obvious love and respect felt by all those present for this unique artist and woman.

After I had transcribed and edited the manuscript, *The Memoirs of Sylvia Olden Lee, Premier African American Classical Vocal Coach* (Lee and Nash 2001). Her life-long friend, colleague, and collaborator William Warfield contributed the Preface, and Patricia wrote the Introduction. On April 10, 2004, Sylvia Olden Lee passed away in Philadelphia, but her exceptional life story had been preserved for all to read. She was the first African American hired onto the staffs of both the Metropolitan Opera and the Curtis Institute of Music. In addition, she was the world's leading authority on the Spiritual. The book contains remarkable tales of her ancestors, one of whom was a Cherokee on the Trail of Tears March.

On February 19, 2017, New York's Harlem Opera Theater sponsored a concert of arias and ensembles at the Schomburg Center for Research in Black Culture honoring Mrs. Lee. The performers were both her distinguished African American colleagues as well as members of the Harlem Opera. I was invited to be the keynote speaker to discuss our writing of her *Memoirs*. Then, on June 27, 2017, New York's Schiller Institute and Harlem Opera Theater presented a gala concert of soloists and chorus celebrating Mrs. Lee at Carnegie Hall. Once again, I was invited to serve as keynote speaker to talk about our joint authorship of Mrs. Lee's *Memoirs*. Towards the end of the evening event, a representative of Mayor Bill de Blasio announced that June 27, 2017 was officially proclaimed "Sylvia Olden Lee Day in New York." The audience of over 2,000 enthusiastic attendees cheered the announcement.

Also, in 1995, we had arranged an interview with the pioneering opera diva Camilla Williams. She was the first African American to receive a regular contract with a major American opera company (the New York City Opera), the first African American to perform a leading role at the Vienna State Opera, the first African American instructor at the Central Conservatory of Music in Beijing, China, and the first African American professor of voice at Indiana University's prestigious School of Music.

When Patricia first contacted Miss Williams, she immediately wanted to know what we both had published. Patricia mentioned her own two discographies on recordings of African American classical singers and my three biographies, the first of which was on the Metropolitan opera star Geraldine Farrar (Nash 2012). "Geraldine Farrar!" exclaimed Miss Williams. "She was my mentor and friend who opened the door to my career in concerts and opera. You can interview me this afternoon if you wish!"

On the day of the interview in Bloomington, IN, Patricia was not well, and I conducted it on my own. We began our recorded discussion of Miss Williams life and career in her beautiful condominium, containing a lifetime of fascinating photos. After lunch in a local restaurant, we moved to her memorabilia-enriched studio in the main instruction and administration building of Indiana University's prestigious School of Music. She was a charismatic raconteur, and she generously shared a wealth of inspiring experiences with me. Miss Williams was a kind, warm person who was able to put the stranger completely at ease. In addition, she was very articulate and organized.

She began to talk of growing up in Virginia with loving, religious parents and siblings. Her mother taught her children "the love of God." They all sang in the church choir and studied piano. After graduating from Virginia State College, Miss Williams was the first and second recipient of the Marian Anderson Award and remained friends with Miss Anderson until the famous contralto's death in 1993.

Geraldine Farrar heard Miss Williams in a concert and immediately used her professional connections to open the concert and opera fields for her. Camilla Williams made her debut as Puccini's Madama Butterfly at the New York City Opera in 1946. The roles of Nedda in Leoncavallo's *Pagliacci,* Mimi in Puccini's *La bohème* and Verdi's Aïda followed. In 1951, she was featured as Bess by Columbia Records in the first complete recording of Gershwin's *Porgy and Bess.* The recording was awarded an Emmy. In 1954, she performed *Madama Butterfly* with London's Sadlers Wells Opera and at the Vienna State Opera, where she was the first African American to appear in a leading role. Moreover, she was a distinguished concert artist who performed all over the world, including fourteen African countries under the sponsorship of the U. S. Department of State. In 1963, she sang "The Star-Spangled Banner" at the Lincoln Memorial before Dr. Martin Luther King Jr.'s "I Have a Dream" speech. By now I realized the importance of Miss Williams' story being made known again. The interview was published in *The Opera Quarterly* (Nash 2002).

Camilla Williams and I remained in touch and soon became friends. She was a wise councilor to me, as Geraldine Farrar had been to her. The long-awaited recognition of her career was beginning to appear when on February 11, 2009 the New York City Opera and the Schomburg Center for Research in Black Culture presented a gala evening in her honor. The *Opera Quarterly* interview of Miss Williams was used as a resource by the New York City Opera for the event. That same year, Camilla Williams was awarded Indiana University's President's Medal for Excellence.

Nevertheless, I was concerned that her life story had not been recorded. But in 2010, I found an online dissertation based on Miss Williams' career by a young Nigerian ethnomusicology student at Indiana University (Shonekan 2003). Dr. Stephanie Shonekan was now a professor of ethnomusicology at Chicago's Columbia College. I ordered a copy and discovered in the subject matter fifty pages of autobiographical writing concluding with Camilla Williams's debut at the New York City Opera.

I phoned Miss Williams who told me that Dr. Shonekan was unable to find a publisher. I had some suggestions which might help in creating an autobiography. I heard from Dr. Shonekan and advised her to record the remainder of Miss Williams's life story and to focus the dissertation as an autobiography. She did and sent me a copy of the revised manuscript to read. It was fascinating, and I recommended it to my publisher as an ideal companion work to *The Memoirs of Sylvia Olden Lee, Premier African American Classical Vocal Coach.* They read the manuscript and offered Miss Williams and Dr. Schonekan a book contract.

The Life of Camilla Williams, African American Classical Singer and Opera Diva (Williams and Schonekan 2011).

At the time of her death on January 29, 2012, *The New York Times* reporter Margalit Fox (2012) wrote a full-page obituary for Miss Williams with her photo in the center of the front page. Ms. Fox had requested permission to quote from my interview in *The Opera Quarterly* (Nash 2012), which again served as a resource for information on Miss Williams's life and career. Ms. Fox and *The New York Times* finally set the record straight about her unique contribution to the opera world and did not miss any key elements of her life story. She indeed had opened the door for Miss Anderson and all of the other future African American opera stars. Both *The New York Times* and London's *The Times* included in their obituaries Miss Williams's statement:

> The lack of recognition for my accomplishments used to bother me, but you cannot cry over these things. There is no place for bitterness in singing. It works on the cords and ruins the voice. In His own good time, God brings everything right. (Fox 2012)

Camilla Williams and I had often talked of Geraldine Farrar since it was her mentorship of Miss Williams and my biography which brought us together. I realized that the final chapter of the biography needed to be revised to include the story of Miss Farrar's mentorship of and friendship with Miss Williams from 1946 until Miss Farrar's death in 1967. Our discussions also led to the addition of a section entitled, "Conversations on Geraldine Farrar with Camilla Williams" in the Appendices of my revised second edition biography, *Geraldine Farrar: Opera's Charismatic Innovator* (Nash 2012).

Note

1. Unless otherwise noted, all quotations are personal communication, given as a form of oral history.

Disclosure statement

No potential conflict of interest was reported by the author.

References

Fox, Margalit. 2012. Camilla Williams, Barrier-Breaking Opera Star, Dies at 92. *The New York Times*, February 2. https://www.nytimes.com/2012/02/03/arts/music/camilla-williams-opera-singer-dies-at-92.html.

Kozinn, Allan. 1993. "Marian Anderson is Dead at 96; Singer Shattered Racial Barriers." *The New York Times*, April 9. https://www.nytimes.com/1993/04/09/obituaries/marian-anderson-is-dead-at-96-singer-shattered-racial-barriers.html.

Lee, Sylvia Olden, and Elizabeth Nash. 2001. *The Memoirs of Sylvia Olden Lee, Premier African American Classical Vocal Coach: Who is Sylvia*. Lewiston, NY: Edwin Mellen Press.

Nash, Elizabeth. 2001. *Autobiographical Reminiscences of African American Classical Singers, 1853-Present: Introducing Their Spiritual Heritage into the Concert Repertoire*. Lewiston, NY: Edwin Mellen Press.

Nash, Elizabeth. 2002. "A Day with Camilla Williams." *The Opera Quarterly* 18 (2): 219–230.

Nash, Elizabeth. 2012. *Geraldine Farrar, Opera's Charismatic Innovator*. 2nd ed. Jefferson, NC: McFarland Press.

Opera North. 1997. "Sylvia Olden Lee's 80th Birthday." Program Notes, June 29.

Shonekan, Stephanie. 2003. "One Life Two Voices: The Examination, Exploration, and Exposition of the Life of Camilla Williams, Soprano." PhD diss., Indiana University.

Williams, Camilla, and Stephanie Schonekan. 2011. *The Life of Camilla Williams, African American Classical Singer and Opera Diva*. Lewiston, NY: Edwin Mellen Press.

Singing Vocal Pedagogy in the Nineteenth Century Neapolitan School: The Work of Francesco Florimo

Giovanna Carugno and Cristina Patturelli

ABSTRACT

This article discusses Francesco Florimo, one of the most important representatives of the nineteenth century Neapolitan music school, and it explores his impact on singing vocal pedagogy history. Florimo notably contributed to the development of the library of the "San Pietro a Majella" Conservatory of Naples, and he is also known for his commitment to teaching generations of singers. Nevertheless, he is less recognized for his contributions to vocal pedagogy history. Completed in 1825 and published several times during the nineteenth century, *Breve metodo di canto* is his treatise on vocal pedagogy, and it summarizes his teaching method. This text was an innovative contribution to voice education; the book not only explored the art of singing, but it also advanced specific elements of voice training that are important to modern singing techniques such as breathing, sound emission, and articulation. The text also provides additional information on the history of human voice and underlines the importance of a progressive approach to the practice of singing, making Florimo an unrecognized forerunner of modern voice education.

Introduction: Francesco Florimo and the Neapolitan Musical School

Francesco Florimo: Biographical Notes

Francesco Florimo was one of the most relevant representatives of the Neapolitan music school of the nineteenth century. Born in 1800 in San Giorgio Morgeto in the Calabria region, he discovered a talent for music in his early childhood; his uncle played the harpsichord, and Florimo followed (Megali Del Giudice 1901). His talent developed during his formal training, starting at the age of 17 in Naples. Through a scholarship, he attended the "San Sebastiano" Conservatory, which later combined with the "San Pietro a Majella" institution (Amministrazione Comunale of San Giorgio Morgeto 1992).

Florimo had the opportunity to be a student of the great composer Niccolò Antonio Zingarelli, who also taught Vincenzo Bellini; Florimo later dedicated a symphony and a hymn to Zingarelli (Cafiero 1997). Florimo specialized under the guidance of other renowned musical masters, such as Giacomo Tritto for counterpoint, Giuseppe Elia for piano, and Giovanni Furno for harmony (Scialò 2017). Moreover, he refined his singing abilities, studying with the famous castrato, Girolamo Crescentini, who was remembered for being one of the best interpreters of the operas by Domenico Cimarosa. Florimo trained not only as a musician and composer, but also as an archivist, music historian, and pedagogue, and he graduated in 1823 with a graduate diploma in conducting.

As a composer, Florimo concentrated on several styles of chamber music, composing secular cantatas and romances with piano accompaniment and also sacred music, which had interested him since the first lessons he attended at the Conservatory (Iesué 2002; Seller 2002). In fact, while still a student, he composed two masses under his master's guidance: a "*Te Deum, a Dixit, a Credo*" and a symphony (De Rosa 1840, 243).

Some years later, his talent for sacred music emerged in the funeral symphony he wrote for his close friend Bellini in 1835, with which he had much success: it was transcribed for solo piano and for four hands by Florimo in 1836, and it was elaborated into a new symphony for Count Wenzel Robert von Gallenberg, performed in 1839 at the "San Pietro a Majella" Conservatory. He also developed two works by Nicola de Giosa: the prayer *Una lacrima sulla tomba del conte di Gallenberg* and a funeral hymn for four voices, choir, and orchestra (Antolini 1988).

These significant works represent the social circles that connected Florimo with other leading figures of nineteenth Neapolitan music. His friendship with Bellini was fundamentally important and mutually beneficial for the two composers, and the friendship added to his renown (Megali Del Giudice 1901). They had copious correspondence that he self-published (Florimo 1882). Florimo strongly promoted their legacy, including a book with piano pieces by the contemporaries of Florimo (Grande 2001) and a slim volume with writings in memory of Bellini (Caroccia 2004a, 57; Darcours 1886).[1]

Along with Bellini, Florimo exchanged letters with other eminent contemporaries (Caroccia 2004b; Seller 2005). In most cases, the correspondence was as the librarian of the "San Pietro a Majella" Conservatory, such as Giuseppe Verdi, the impresario Domenico Barbaja, Giuseppe Saverio Mercadante, Gaetano Braga, and Lauro Rossi (Grande 2005; Marvin Montemorra 2013; Schlitzer 1946; Walker 1945; Rosselli 1985; Caroccia 2005a).[2] These letters are invaluable historical and bibliographical sources, which make it possible to link the social, cultural, and artistic musical world of the nineteenth century (Caroccia 2005b, xxix). In this sense, Florimo's correspondence provides not only a sketch of the personal life of the composer and his friends, but also information on the musical development during that time (Caroccia 2005b, xxix).

In addition, Florimo was a celebrated archivist, devoted to enlarging the collections of the "San Pietro a Majella" Conservatory. Succeeding Giuseppe Sigismondo, Florimo served from 1827 to 1881. He died from pneumonia and was replaced by his pupil Rocco Edoardo Pagliara, who at the time was the administrative director of the library (Giammattei 2003).[3] Thanks to Florimo, the archive of the "San Pietro a Majella" Conservatory archive became one of the most important in Europe, distinguished for its large collection of works from composers throughout Europe (Lombardo 2016).

Moreover, Florimo was the author of a pivotal historical work on the Neapolitan music school and the conservatories of Naples: La *scuola musicale di Napoli e i suoi Conservatori, con uno sguardo sulla storia della musica in Italia* (Florimo 1881–1883). It was published in four volumes over three years, constituting an extended version of a previous work, titled *Cenno storico sulla scuola musicale di Napoli* (Florimo 1861).[4]

Due to Florimo's business savvy in his musical career[5] and his commitment to popularizing the Neapolitan music school, he was aptly named the "Nestor" of the musical field (Masutto 1882, 74), and he is unquestionably one of most influential musicians of nineteenth century in Italy (Fétis 1878). During his life, Florimo was awarded various commendations,[6] and he was appointed as a member of prestigious *accademie* in both Naples with the "Pontiniana" Academy in 1890, and the Royal Academy of Archeology, Humanities and Fine Arts, in 1883. And he was honored in other important Italian musical centers such as the *accademie filarmoniche* of Bologna, Palermo, Catania, and Messina (Amministrazione Comunale of San Giorgio Morgeto 1992; Basso 1985). From 1835 until his death, he was also artistic director of the Philharmonic Society of Naples.

Francesco Florimo's Contributions to the Neapolitan Music School

The Neapolitan music school highlights the city of Naples's relevance to European musical history (Cafiero 2005b). When looking at the history of the "glorious" Neapolitan music school (as it was called), it is important to note that not all of the musicians and composers at the school were Neapolitans (Spadea 2008). As Giulia Veneziano (2017) highlighted, the "peculiarly Neapolitan style [...] traced the history of musicographical and musicological traditions," to the point that also the "modern scholars still tend to associate the Neapolitan provenance of music and its most prominent composers with an assumed common style, for which the appropriate term remains, as before, 'Neapolitan'" (206). In other words, being from the Neapolitan school related more to a style of music rather than a specific geography. This style was primarily described as a compositional one, which specifically related to counterpoint (Burney 1789, 544).[7] And it influenced the development of the opera, in particular the *opera comica*, not only in Italy, but also in "other nations, and for many successive years the well-earned reputation of the school was maintained by their pupils" (Kiesewetter 2013, 221).

In the La *scuola musicale di Napoli e i suoi Conservatori*, Florimo defined the Neapolitan school as the most ancient of Italian schools (Florimo 1881–1883). It began during the middle of the fifteenth century by the Flemish composer Giovanni Tinctoris, named as *kapellmeister* by the king of Aragon, Ferdinand I (Florimo 1881–1883, 27).[8] Florimo was vital in preserving the history of the school and its legacy. And arguably, the Neapolitan school begins modern music history (Schlüter 1865).

Vocal Technique in the Nineteenth Century

Francesco Florimo's contribution to vocal pedagogy must be understood within its historical context and within the singing aesthetic of the nineteenth century, which rapidly changed because of the popularity of opera and the changing tastes of its audiences. Because of these varying tastes, the concept of "correct" singing was always in flux (Patalini 2015).

In the middle of the nineteenth century, there were several medical discoveries in the field of phoniatrics that helped to advance vocal pedagogy: the invention of the laryngoscope in 1854 by the Spanish singing master Manuel García and the birth of the field of logopedics (Radomski 2000). With these advances, the importance of the diaphragmatic and abdominal breathing started to be stressed in most works on singing. To "breathe is to sing and to sing is to breathe" (Smith and Sataloff 2012, vii). This concept underlined a concept already in practice in the eighteenth century by Tosi (1723) and Mancini (1777), which came from the bel canto tradition but with different aims. The bel canto tradition emphasized breathing "higher" in the thorax. This "natural" breathing, as proposed by the belcantists, comes from a singing course textbook at the Paris Conservatoire at the beginning of the nineteenth century.[9] The breathing they advocated is deeper than the one used for the speech and involves the chest raising (inhalation) and lowering (exhalation), which is said to support the vocal sound with the air pressure to the diaphragm (so-called "breath support" or *appoggio* technique).

In 1856, phoniatric Louis Mandl contested this breathing technique and called it dangerous for the voice. He did not advocate chest raising and "remarked the importance of the low larynx" (Stark 2003, 40). This new method of breathing also included other concepts in vocal technique.[10] It emphasized the significance of tongue position and other aspects such as "the lip modifications, the shortening or elongation of the cavity of articulation, and the great resulting variety of vibrations," especially to reach a perfect intonation of the vowels, both "in singing [and] in speaking" (as quoted by Sell 2017, 11). This different and (for the time) more scientific approach to vocal technique continued to advance in the following years, to the point that "in the last quarter of the nineteenth century many teaching concepts came directly from the rapidly developing [fields] of the science in acoustics and phonetics" (Mason 2000, 215).

Breve Metodo Di Canto by Francesco Florimo

Introduction

Up to 1800, singing pedagogy was largely an oral tradition, particularly since there was little awareness of vocal physiology that could be shared in a written form. Francesco Florimo was among the first to write an educational text that focuses on vocal anatomy and its functioning, titled *Breve metodo di canto*. This treatise, completed in 1825, is divided into three parts and was printed several times by different publishers during the nineteenth century. A second edition of the treatise, published by Ricordi in 1840, contained a fourth part dedicated to Gioacchino Rossini.

Subsequently, a series of other works on singing by various authors were published, considering the importance of voice training. The manuscript of Florimo, kept at the "San Pietro a Majella" Conservatory of Naples, consists of the text and an enclosed leaflet. In the treatise, the author—in order to prepare the singer to face difficulties—introduces himself as a lover of the old vocal traditions. He said he also wished to connect singers with the art of music and the ancient of music beauty that lasted forever and at the same time teach Baroque singing styles, which he said would "obscure and cover with oblivion" (Florimo 1840a, 1, 1840b, 5).[11]

Florimo's work joined the debate that appeared at his time about vocal teaching: as vocal anatomy started attracting the attention of musicians, the question became how to make the knowledge in the vocal physiology useful to teaching methodologies and ideas (Göpfert 1988). For this reason, *Breve metodo di canto* had significant success: it was awarded at the Universal Exhibition in Paris in 1877 and at the National Exhibition in Milan in 1881. And the book was judged "magistral" by Gioacchino Rossini, who endorsed it for a long time at the Paris Conservatory where he was teacher; Rossini's singing school was always very strict and demanding, and the school praised the book with a resolution on March 6, 1866. In addition, the *Gazzetta musicale di Milano* mentioned *Breve metodo di canto* as the best treatise on singing.

Structure and Aims of the Treatise

The first pages of the treatise *Breve metodo di canto* provide specific methodological suggestions that only in the edition by Ricordi; this is preserved at the library of the "San Pietro a Majella" Conservatory of Naples, and they are catalogued under the title *Teorie preliminari* (Preliminary theories) with the aim to introduce the student to basic concepts and theories on singing (Florimo 18 40b, 5). However, the contents of this first section are vague and lack any reference to the physiological and scientific aspects of a singing technique. Nevertheless, the work does have important value. Florimo does not provide detailed instructions; however, he was to capture "the progress that the art of singing has done on its own" (*I progressi che l'arte del canto ha fatto ai dì nostri*) (Florimo 1840a, 2). He asserts that the production of the voice happens in the larynx, but he does not offer a codified theory of singing.

Thus, he continues to deepen the technical and aesthetical aspects of singing by writing a chapter mainly addressed to teachers and titled *Metodo da osservarsi nel dare lazioni di canto* (*Method to be Observed in Giving Lessons of Singing*). The chapter is divided into three sections:

- breathing;
- vocalization; and
- how to "spin" and "bring the voice."

This chapter is followed by another, which discusses music and provides an illustrative table about voice registers. From a historical perspective, Florimo's treatise is perfectly placed in the tradition of the Italian singing school, arguing that the singer should not separate vocal education from the development of the musicianship and ear training such as *solfeggio*.

Looking at technique specifically, *Breve metodo di canto* is divided into four parts, each of them allows the student to gradually face various levels of difficulty, from an easy beginning exercise to those of great vocal agility. The first part presents exercises on the intervals of major third, minor third, fourth, fifth, etc., and there are exercises for intonation and a series of *solfeggio*. The second part is dedicated to the musical "scale volate" (scales to be sung quickly and with extreme agility) and to with agility ornamentation such as trills and the gruppetto. The third part contains 24 *solfeggio* exercises including a series of melodies, and the fourth part includes only agility exercises and *solfeggio*.

The Art of Singing in Breve metodo di canto

Before writing his treatise, Florimo evaluated the best works on singing published at his time, collecting the information he considered most useful. Florimo's goal was to simplify the various methodologies and improve them for all voice types; in this, he included a short book addressed to all learners. Florimo argues that if a good voice is a natural gift then strong training improves it. Conversely, straining the voice or altering it in a harmful way only tends to ruin it. At the same time, ensuring and being certain of a student's specific vocal register is paramount, so Florimo provides a table which illustrates the various vocal registers, which is divided into high, less high, low, and less low.

Florimo argued that teachers must correctly evaluate each student examining vocal register, natural extension, and other health conditions and pathologies; this is the first step of every grounded teaching method. In his view, student should not vainly try to acquire what is not in their natural abilities, or they risk ruining and damaging their vocal instrument. Florimo made this point clear.

Florimo was one of the first teachers on record to argue that the voice (phonation) did *not* occur from the chest, head, or frontal sinuses (Florimo 1840). As is scientifically accurate, he taught that the voice (phonation) is produced in the larynx, and he taught that it is necessary to have control over the laryngeal muscles. The "inspired" air enters the lungs, and an individual's "will" produces the voice through the exhaled air (Florimo 1840, 2).[12] Florimo understood then what modern scientific research has affirmed: phonation is in part a cognitive process.

However rudimentary, Florimo introduced the basic parameters of the voice, providing brief and elementary notions of acoustics. He mentions the concept of frequency by claiming that the voices are subdivided into more or less low or into more or less high, and this difference depends on the number of oscillations in a given period of time. Florimo also notes elements of vocal style, and he matches many modern criteria for modern vocal artistry. For example, he correctly believed that the throat and nose can cause defects in singing, either acquired because of poor training or from pathologies in the nasal cavities, soft palate, or other areas of resonance.

Additionally, while not necessarily scientifically accurate, he also argued that each voice has three registers (the register of low sounds, the register of the middle sounds, and the register of high sounds), and he described the different gradation of each sound as either strong, soft, and sweet. He believed that this was a consequence of putting more or less strength in "spreading" the voice, introducing what he defined as "intensity." Additionally, Florimo meticulously studied the *passaggio* (the part of the vocal extension between two registers of a singer), and he provided exercises to guide the voice and train it to bridge the two vocal registers. This emphasis in the *passaggio* is noteworthy and mirrors many modern aesthetic choices in opera training today.

Florimo's educational process is based on repetition and internalizing theoretical and practical concepts. The exercises should eventually feel automatic, and students should be able to sing them in various vocal registers. In 1889, the *Gazzetta musicale di Milano* underlined the importance of Florimo's work. They noted that until *Breve metodo di canto* was published singing teachers did not consider physiology; rather, they merely required students to perform various scales and arpeggios without explanation or in method in many cases. Florimo was the first academic singing authority to give anatomic explanations for his exercises proposed, and he gave a clear methodology to singing training.

Florimo's ideas were so modern that many of his concepts seem fundamental to singing training to teachers today. For example, he taught that posture was important for the singer and that diction and pronunciation were elements of aesthetics and style in singing training. He also taught that the body should be in a "natural" state while singing. He believed that tense muscles, unaligned postures, and forced expressions lead to compromised voiced health. These ideas were immensely innovative for the nineteenth century, and they are often still taught today.

Many of Florimo's ideas on posture are particularly noteworthy. To begin, Florimo claims that students must stand in front of the teacher during the lesson, in order to let the teacher see and correct the defects. The teacher should take care that the student stands naturally straight and does not make the least [unnatural] effort or movement (Florimo 1840a, 3, 1840b, 6).[13] In order not to feel stress during the vocal lesson, the student should assume the following physiological posture: the feet should be slightly apart about the width of the shoulders; the knees should not be hypertensive or bent, but softly stretched; the torso should be erect and relaxed with broad shoulders; the physiological lumbar and cervical curves should not be altered; and the head should be raised and not inclined to one side (Florimo 1840a, 3, 1840b, 6).[14] Florimo was the first teacher on record to give this kind of postural specification in voice training.

About Breathing

In the nineteenth century, singing teachers generally neglected the importance of the breath in training. While breathing is often debated in pedagogy, the relationship to breathing and health and its importance to training is well documented (Hoch 2017). Additionally, breathing has stylistic relevance for a singer. Florimo affirmed this stylistic significance and encouraged singers to feel free to breath at their pleasure at first, regardless of particular musical phrases or words and without considering the expressive meaning of the musical composition. The use of the breath can be trained, and the *Breve metodo di canto* provides exercises to enhance this ability. According to Florimo, breathing must be performed without someone noticing it, with the exception of a "breath of expression" as he called it. This kind of breathing can be distinguished in (1) "whole breath" in which the breath can be taken in the rests, at the end of the musical phrase before a long note and corresponding to a "crowned point," and (2) "half-breath," also called "stolen breath" (Florimo 1840a, 4, 1840b, 7). Half-breath should be taken carefully after a long note, before an ornamentation, after the first period of a musical phrase, and often in the middle of long agility passages, where should be completely concealed not to compromise a good execution of the passages themselves.

About Vocalization

In the context of Florimo's pedagogy, vocalization consists of singing vowels. Florimo considered the vowel/a/as the most suitable to do any exercise. The mouth must always be constantly open and smiling, and the chin, tongue, and the lips should not move.

This is the only way to create a correct "vocalism" and to avoid extraneous muscle tension. He also advocated for what modern pedagogues may term a "mid laryngeal positional," where the larynx is neither raised nor lowered. Florimo, in the three parts of his treatise, provides detailed explanations and exercises dedicated to stylistic vocal refinement, which includes:

messa di voce,
- resonation,
- pronunciation,
- vocal registers, which Florimo illustrates in table form,
- concepts to give to the voice different effects, such as moving from pianissimo to fortissimo and how to manage the different dynamics.[15]

The first part of *Breve metodo di canto* contains exercises to assure what he would consider correct and the pure intonation of all the intervals, in order to facilitate musical interpretation and improve musicianship (Florimo 1840a, 10). For example, he offered:

- 22 lessons focused on the low scale in order to address resonance, pitch, and uniformity of tone,
- 10 exercises to train intonation of intervals, from the third up to the twelfth,
- 9 other exercises to be performed in *lento, moderato*, and *allegro* time on intervals from the third to the eleventh, and
- *solfeggio* exercises.

In each section the teacher has to give direct instruction and monitor progress. According to Florimo, shrewd teachers do not move to a new exercise unless the student has perfected the previous one. Each exercise should be always performed strictly *lento, moderato* and *allegro* (Florimo 1840a, 30).[16]

The second part of Florimo's treatise focuses on purely stylistic exercises that assume a high level of technical singing proficiency. The exercises are mainly vocal scales and kinds of ornamentation. The 24 exercises are a progression that should be performed with both strong articulation and with *legato* sing throughout the entire vocal tract and without moving the chin or lips (Florimo 1840a, 5). There are 12 other exercises that address other stylistic components (Florimo 1840a, 59), such as various ornamentations like trills, syncopation, chromatic scales, and vocal registration (Florimo 1840a, 111).

The third part of the *Breve metodo di canto* is composed of *solfeggio* exercises that augment other technical and stylistic vocal skills. In this section, Florimo uses a variety of melodies (Swedish, English, Circassia [modern day Turkish], Spanish, and Neapolitan) to give the singer to confidence in interpreting different musical styles. This eclectic approach is noteworthy and unique for its time.

The fourth part of the treatise focuses on agility, vocal extension, and tonal consistency throughout different registers (Florimo 1840b). Teachers were welcome to have students vary tempo and tonal quality. According to Florimo, teachers could vary singing elements at this point in a student's individual training as long as the goal of each exercise was clear and as long as the student moved in a logical progression (Florimo 1840b).

The Impact of the *Breve metodo di canto* on Vocal Education in the Nineteenth Century

The treatise *Breve metodo di canto* by Francesco Florimo had a significant impact on vocal education training during the second half of the nineteenth century for a variety of reasons. First, Florimo was a well-known and prolific teacher who taught piano and singing for almost 30 years in the city of Naples. He created a legacy of "progressive" teaching, and he created a systematic and methodical style of teaching that was unique for its time (Lombardo 2016). In this sense, Florimo combined a practical approach with a theoretical one; he gave his pupils a more complete knowledge on the art of singing and anticipated many current vocal education trends and focus on fact-based and science-based vocal pedagogy styles.

Nevertheless, he continued many Medieval traditions such as publishing a treatise that includes both exercises and repertoire. Like his predecessors, Florimo included *solfeggio* exercises that should be studied before performing a song accompanied by the piano; this was already a part of the traditional vocal training in the Neapolitan music school since the eighteenth century (Sullo 2017).[17] Because of this unique blend of traditional and pioneering methods, *Breve metodo di canto* was immensely successful during Florimo's life and many singing teachers used the text, not only in Italy but also throughout Europe and beyond (Chemi 2002; Costa 1882).

Final Remarks

Florimo's *Breve metodo di canto* provides important information on the art of singing and training in the Neapolitan music school during second half of nineteenth century. The treatise was appreciated and adopted as a textbook in almost all the conservatories in Italy and beyond the Alps, such as in Berlin, London, and Saint Petersburg, and the book had immense academic renown because of its exhaustive practical advice on breathing technique and the way acoustics and vocal anatomy were presented. The method developed by Florimo offered many artists and teachers the opportunity to have singing lessons in a simple and effective way, particularly for the time period.

Unfortunately, Florimo's legacy has been too often lost in the history of singing pedagogy.

While there were other texts on vocal education, particularly from the students of Giuseppe Aprili such as Lablache, Garcia, and Crescentini, these authors were inspired by the work of Florimo, and they considering his works a point of reference for their own treatises. Thus, at the very least, Florimo was a founder of many seminal concepts of modern vocal technique. He predates many contemporary ideas of combining singing training with vocal physiology and scientific detail, which is an education staple to many modern teachers today. Thus, *Breve metodo di canto* remains a viable educational resource for basic vocal technique, where many of the concepts have been solidified and proven through modern advances. Ultimately, Florimo was not only a musician, archivist, and a music historian as he is often thought, but he is also a forerunner of the modern voice education, and future generations of singers and teachers should regard him as such.[18]

Notes

1. Florimo helped to develop a "myth" around Bellini by censoring the content of his letters supporting building of a monument in his honor. See Maione (2001, 2004) and Cavalleri (2017).
2. Florimo's esteem for the composer from Busseto is demonstrated also by the fact that he sent him the first volume of his work *Cenno storico sulla scuola musicale di Napoli*, writing: "Without being either a man of science or a man of letters, I have ventured to write a book. If the world only regards my good intentions, then it will have indulgence for me, otherwise I shall be lost" (Libby and Rosselli 2001).
3. Florimo proposed to establish a music museum connected to the archive of the Conservatory with different areas for diverse instruments; it was organized by period, function, and musical characteristic (Ruta 1877; Cafiero 1997).
4. The first volume of the work—titled *Come venne* La *musica in Italia ed origine delle scuole italiane*—describes the evolution of music in Italy, starting with sacred music in the Medieval era and moving to the different musical "schools" (Neapolitan, Bolognian, Lombard, Venetian, Roman, and Florentina). In the second and third volumes, Florimo traces the birth and development of the various conservatories. The last volume of the work contains a brief overview on the theatrical venues of the city of Naples and the operas that were staged there. (Florimo 1881–1883).
5. Florimo also worked as a composer and copyist transcribing operas for the Neapolitan publisher Girard (Caroccia 2005b, XXXV). After his death, the works by Florimo were published—by means of an ad hoc agreement—in various collections by Ricordi and Lucca (Plenizio 2009).
6. In 1869 Florimo became an officer, and in 1887 a great official of the Order of the Italian Crown. He also received the Commenda of Saint Maurizio and Lazzaro, the Grand Cross of Saint Michele from Baviera, and the medal of Simone Bolivar (Amministrazione Comunale of San Giorgio Morgeto 1992).
7. According to Florimo, the rules of the counterpoint are the same in all schools. What differentiate one form the other is the methods of teaching, the use of some harmonic combinations, and the desired musical effects. The music created by the composers of the Neapolitan school is characterized by naturalness, real expression, and vivacity of the feelings communicated through the sounds (Florimo 1881–1883).
8. The origins of the Neapolitan music school are still controversial today, due to different masters and to the diverse eras of evolution of the Neapolitan style (Cafiero 2005a). If Florimo dated them back to the Renaissance era, some contemporary scholars affirm that it was developed "towards the close of the seventeenth century" thanks to the composer Alessandro Scarlatti (Gurney 2011, 465).
9. The reference is made to the *Méthode de chant Du Conservatoire de musique contenant les principes Du chant, Des exercices pour La voix, Des solfèges tirés Des meilleurs ouvrages anciens et modernes et Des airs dans tous les mouvements et les différents caractères*, elaborated in 1803 by an ad hoc commission that the Italian singer Bernardo Mengozzi also participated in (Hondré 1996).
10. In this sense, breathing technique was an innovative perspective for vocal education. Since until the nineteenth century, this element was often neglected, due to both the inexperience of the masters and the negligence of the pupils (Crivelli 1820).
11. The full Italian translation is "Richiamare alla memoria degli amatori della musica quell'antico bello che dura eterno, perchè e invano la moda barocca del giorno si affatica ad oscurare e coprire d'oblio."
12. The full Italian translation is "La voce viene prodotta nella laringe, e perché si produca è necessario che la volontà concorra a modificare questo organo vocale. L'aria inspirata entra nei polmoni ed il concorso della volontà ingenera la voce attraverso l'aria espirata."

13. The full Italian translation is "È necessario che l'allievo durante la lezione sia di fronte al maestro, affinché veda e corregga i difetti bisogna aver cura che l'allievo stia diritto naturalmente non faccio il minimo sforzo o movimento."
14. The full Italian translation is "*Senza che si inclini da alcun lato il che impedirebbe alla voce di uscire in tutta La sua naturale estensione.*"
15. The full Italian translation is "La *messa di voce; modo di fila relegare portare La voce della pronunzia una tavola illustrativa dei Registri vocali dei segni convenzionali per dare La voce effetti diversi dal pianissimo al fortissimo; in che modo devono essere gestite le diverse dinamiche.*"
16. The full Italian translation is "*L'accorto maestro non passi ad un nuovo esercizio, se l'allievo non avrà acquisito un certo grado di perfezione e di sicurezza nel precedente, eseguire sempre al rigore di tempo lento poi moderato ed in ultimo allegro.*"
17. Solfeggio exercises aimed at "improving the flexibility of the voice" and reinforced a variety of technical abilities from dynamics to articulation. They were "long and complex exercises, similar in style to the exercises written for instrumentalists, without lyrics, intended to be performed on an open vowel such as Ah, Eh or Oo [/a/,/i/,/o/] or the sol-fa syllables Do, Re, Mi, Fa, Sol, La, Si, Do" (Robertson-Kirkland 2013, 4).
18. This paper is the product of a joint collaboration between the two authors. Cristina Patturelli authored the paragraphs titled "*Breve Metodo di Canto* by Francesco Florimo" and "Final remarks." Giovanna Carugno is the author of the remaining paragraphs.

Disclosure statement

No potential conflict of interest was reported by the authors.

References

Amministrazione Comunale of San Giorgio Morgeto. 1992. *Note biografiche su Francesco Florimo*. Reggio Calabria: Jason.

Antolini, Bianca Maria. 1988. "De Giosa, Nicola." In *Dizionario biografico degli italiani*, edited by Istituto dell'Enciclopedia italiana, Vol. 36 349–353. Rome: Istituto dell'enciclopedia italiana. Accessed June 1, http://www.treccani.it/enciclopedia/nicola-de-giosa_(Dizionario-Biografico).

Basso, Alberto. 1985. "Florimo, Francesco." In *Vol. 2 of Dizionario enciclopedico universale della musica e dei musicisti*, edited by Alberto Basso. *Le biografie*, 783–784. Turin: Utet.

Burney, Charles. 1789. *A General History of Music from the Earliest Ages to the Present Period*. London: Burney.

Cafiero, Rosa. 1997. "Florimo, Francesco." In *Dizionario biografico degli italiani*, edited by Istituto dell'Enciclopedia italiana, 349–353. Vol. 48. Rome: Istituto dell'enciclopedia italiana.

Cafiero, Rosa. 2005a. "Carlo Contumaci nella tradizione didattica della 'scuola napoletana'." In *Affetti musicali: Studi in onore di Sergio Martinotti*, edited by Maurizio Padoan, 105–120. Milan: Vita e Pensiero.

Cafiero, Rosa. 2005b. "Conservatories and the Neapolitan School: A European Model at the Dnd of the Eighteenth Century?" In *Vol. 1 Of Music Education in Europe (1770–1914): Compositional, Institutional and Political Challenges*, edited by Michael Fend and Michel Noiray, 15–29. Berlin: Berliner Wissenschafts-Verlag.

Caroccia, Antonio. 2004a. "Florimo e l'Album pianistico di Bellini." In *Vincenzo Bellini nel secondo centenario della nascita: Atti del convegno internazionale*, edited by Graziella Seminara and Anna Tedesco, 57–76. Florence: Olschki.

Caroccia, Antonio. 2004b. *La corrispondenza salvata: Lettere di maestri e compositori a Francesco Florimo*. Palermo: Mnemes.

Caroccia, Antonio. 2005a. "La corrispondenza tra Francesco Florimo e Lauro Rossi." *Fonti musicali italiane* 10: 117–148.

Caroccia, Antonio. 2005b. *I corrispondenti abruzzesi di Florimo. Selezione dall'Epistolario*. Lucca: Libreria musicale italiana.

Cavalleri, Cesare. 2017. "Le lettere di Bellini e il mistero del genio giovane." *Avvenire*, December 27.

Chemi, Tatiana. 2002. "La romanza di Mario Costa: Ricognizione storica e geografica." In *La romanza italiana da salotto*, edited by Francesca Sanvitale, 301–318. Turin: Edt.

Costa, Mario. March 14, 1882. "Letter to Francesco Florimo." *Library of the "San Pietro a Majella" Conservatory of Naples*.

Crivelli, Domenico. 1820. *L'arte del canto ossia corso completo di insegnamento sulla coltivazione della voce*. London: Crivelli.

Darcours, Charles. 1886. "L'Album Bellini." *Le Figaro*, April 18.

De Rosa, Carlo Antonio. 1840. *Memorie dei compositori di musica del Regno di Napoli*. Naples: Stamperia reale.

Fétis, François Joseph. 1878. "Florimo (Francesco)." In *Vol. 1 of the Biographie universelle des musiciens et bibliographie générale de la musique*, edited by François Joseph Fétis. *Supplément et complément*. Paris: Firmin-Didot.

Florimo, Francesco. 1840a. *Breve metodo di canto*. Naples: Girard.

Florimo, Francesco. 1840b. *Metodo di canto composto e dedicato al Cav. Crescentini*. Milan: Ricordi.

Florimo, Francesco. 1861. *Cenno storico sulla scuola musicale di Napoli*. Naples: Roc.

Florimo, Francesco. 1881–1883. *La scuola musicale di Napoli e i suoi Conservatori, con uno sguardo sulla storia della musica in Italia*. Naples: Morano.

Florimo, Francesco. 1882. *Bellini: Memorie e lettere*. Florence: Barbera.

Giammattei, Emma. 2003. *Il romanzo di Napoli: Geografia e storia letteraria nei secoli XIX e XX*. Naples: Guida.

Göpfert, Bernd. 1988. *Handbuch der gesangskunst*. Wilhelmshaven: Noetzel.

Grande, Tiziana. 2001. "L'Album-Bellini di Florimio-Scherillo e l'inaugurazione del monumento a Bellini." In *Francesco Florimo a Vincenzo Bellini*, edited by Dario Miozzi, 123–149. Catania: Maimone.

Grande, Tiziana. 2005. "Lettere dalla biblioteca. La corrispondenza di Francesco Florimo dalla biblioteca di San Pietro a Majella (1886–1888)." In *In Napoli Musicalissima. Studi in onore di Renato Di Benedetto per il suo 70° compleanno*, edited by Enrico Careri and Pier Paolo De Martino, 183–209. Lucca: Libreria musicale italiana.

Gurney, Edmund. 2011. *The Power of Sound*. Cambridge: Cambridge University Press.

Hoch, Matthew. 2017. "The Legacy of William Vennard and D. Ralph Appelman and Their Influence on Singing Voice Pedagogy: Reflections after 50 Years (1967–2017)." *Voice and Speech Review* 11 (3): 308–313. doi:10.1080/23268263.2017.1395591.

Hondré, Emmanuel. 1996. "Le Conservatoire de Paris et le renouveau du chant français." *Romantisme* 93: 83–94. doi:10.3406/roman.1996.3128.

Iesué, Alberto. 2002. "Le canzoni di Francesco Florimo." *Musicaaa! Periodico di cultura musicale* 23: 5–10.

Kiesewetter, Raphael Georg. 2013. *History of the Modern Music of Western Europe*. Cambridge: Cambridge University Press.

Libby, Dennis, and John Rosselli. 2001. "Florimo, Francesco." *The New Grove Dictionary of Music and Musicians*, edited by Stanley Sadie. London: Macmillan. Accessed May 29, http://www.oxfordmusiconline.com/grovemusic/search?q=florimo&searchBtn=Search&isuickSearch=true.

Lombardo, Maria. 2016. "Il maestro Francesco Florimo da San Giorgio Morgeto." Hagia Agathe, Accessed May 27. http://hagiaagathe.blogspot.com/2016/07/il-maestro-francesco-florimo-da-san.html

Maione, Paologiovanni. 2001. "Florimo All'amico Bellini: 'Un Monumento Eterno Di Sospiri, Di Slanci E Di Melodie'." In *Francesco Florimo a Vincenzo Bellini*, edited by Graziella Seminara and Anna Tedesco, 65–122. Catania: Maimone.

Maione, Paologiovanni. 2004. "Le lettere censurate e il culto del collezionismo: Florimo biografo-alchimista." In *Vincenzo Bellini nel secondo centenario della nascita: Atti del convegno internazionale*, edited by Graziella Seminara and Anna Tedesco, 39–56. Florence: Olschki.

Mancini, Giambattista. 1777. *Pensieri e riflessioni pratiche sul canto figurato*. Milan: Galeazzi.

Marvin Montemorra, Roberta. 2013. "Verdi's Music of the Life'." In *Music in Print and Beyond: Hildegard Von Bingen to the Beatles*, edited by Craig Monson and Roberta Montemorra Marvin, 158–179. Rochester: University of Rochester Press.

Mason, David. 2000. "The Teaching (And Learning) of Singing." In *The Cambridge Companion to Singing*, edited by John Potter and Jonathan Cross, 204–220. Cambridge: Cambridge University Press.

Masutto, Giovanni. 1882. *I maestri di musica italiani del secolo XIX: Notizie biografiche raccolte*. Venice: Cecchini.

Megali Del Giudice, Giuseppe. 1901. *Francesco Florimo l'amico di Vincenzo Bellini*. Naples: Diogene.

Patalini, Alessandro. 2015. *La scuola del respiro. Antologia commentata delle testimonianze sulla respirazione nel Belcanto*. Varese: Zecchini.

Plenizio, Gianfranco. 2009. *Lo core sperduto: La tradizione musicale napoletana e la canzone*. Naples: Guida.

Radomski, James Vincent. 2000. *Manuel García: 1775–1832: Chronicle of the Life of a Bel Canto Tenor at the Dawn of Romanticism*. Oxford: Oxford University Press.

Robertson-Kirkland, Brianna. 2013. "The Silencing of Bel Canto." *Esharp* 21 (7): 0–11.

Rosselli, John. 1985. *L'impresario D'opera*. Turin: EDT.

Ruta, Michele. 1877. *Storia critica delle condizioni della musica in Italia e del conservatorio di S. Pietro a Majella di Napoli*. Naples: Detken and Rocholl.

Schlitzer, Franco. 1946. "Il carteggio inedito Verdi-Florimo." *Rassegna d'Italia* 1: 23–40.

Schlüter, Joseph. 1865. *A General History of Music*. London: Bentley.

Scialò, Pasquale. 2017. *Storia della canzone napoletana*. Milan: Neri Pozza.

Sell, Karen. 2017. *The Disciplines of Vocal Pedagogy: Towards an Holistic Approach*. Abingdon: Routledge.

Seller, Francesca. 2002. "Zingarelli, Mercadante, Florimo e la romanza nell'editoria musicale partenopea dell'Ottocento." In *La romanza italiana da salotto*, edited by Francesco Sanvitale, 197–207. Turin: EDT-Istituto nazionale tostiano.

Seller, Francesca. 2005. "Antonio Caroccia, La corrispondenza salvata. Lettere di maestri e compositori a Francesco Fiorirne, Palermo, Mnemes, 2004, pp. 415." *Rivista italiana di musicologia* 40 (1/2): 408.

Smith, Brenda, and Robert Thayer Sataloff. 2012. *Choral Pedagogy and the Older Singer*. Abingdon: Plural Publishing.

Spadea, Roberto. 2008. *Il Conservatorio di San Pietro a Majella*. Naples: Electa.

Stark, James. 2003. *Bel Canto: A History of Vocal Pedagogy*. Toronto: University of Toronto Press.

Sullo, Paolo. 2017. "Il solfeggio napoletano e gli schemi galanti: Una sintesi." In *La cantata da camera e lo stile galante. Sviluppi e diffusione della "nuova musica" tra il 1720 e il 1760*, edited by Giulia Giovani and Stefano Aresi, 193–214. Amsterdam: Stile galante.

Tosi, Pier Francesco. 1723. *Opinioni de' cantori antichi e moderni*. Bologna: Della Volpe.

Veneziano, Giulia. 2017. "Investigations into the Cantata in Naples during the First Half of the Eighteenth Century: The Cantatas by Leonardo Vinci Contained in a 'Neapolitan' Manuscript." In *Aspects of the Secular Cantata in Late Baroque Italy*, edited by Michael Talbot, 203–226. New York: Routledge.

Walker, Frank. 1945. "Verdi and Francesco Florimo: Some Unpublished Letters." *Music and Letters* 26 (4): 201–208. doi:10.1093/ml/26.4.201.

The History of the Voice and Speech Trainers Association (VASTA)

Adrianne Moore

ABSTRACT
This article offers an overview of the history of the Voice and Speech Trainers Association (VASTA). The organization began with five members in the mid-1980s whose interests were in teaching voice and speech primarily for the performing arts, and the society has evolved into a leading force for voice trainers globally across a wide body of fields and interests. The article includes a discussion of the organization's early history, which is followed by a discussion of VASTA's growth and brief overviews of major initiatives throughout the length of the organization.

This article examines the first several decades of the Voice and Speech Trainers Association (VASTA). This account focuses on the major initiatives, achievements, and developments that have taken place since its inception.[1] To begin, I offer a brief overview of the organization:

> The Voice and Speech Trainers Association (VASTA) is an international organization whose mission is to advance the art, research, and visibility of the voice and speech profession. VASTA serves the needs of voice and speech specialists, teachers, scholars, practitioners, coaches, and artists by supporting and empowering those who work and study in the voice field. A multidisciplinary organization, VASTA aims to broaden public understanding of the nature and importance of voice and speech use and training, and VASTA creates opportunities for ongoing education and exchange among the varying voice communities: performing arts, theatre, music, communication, business coaching, linguistics, health, speech science, and others. (Sansom 2018, 9)

Early VASTA History

While VASTA now includes trainers from a variety of fields, it originally developed out of a need to unite voice trainers for theatre actors. The first academic gathering devoted to the actor's vocal training originated in Los Angeles, California, at an American Theatre Association (ATA) convention in 1968. Dorothy Mennen (VASTA's first president) recalls it as "a dynamic session which fired the spark that initiated a new group called Theatre Voice and Speech" (VASTA 1987). This group functioned at the national level and included many of the people who would later play a significant role in the formation of VASTA.

Separately, VASTA formally grew out of the Speech Program of the University and College Theatre Association, the largest division of ATA, and VASTA was officially born in August of 1986 at the National Educational Theatre Conference in New York City.[2] Carol Pendergrast remembers that "in the beginning there were only five women and a waste-basket [to pass around and collect money]" (June 2012).

Carol Pendergrast, Dorothy Mennen, Lucille Rubin, Bonnie Raphael, and Mary Corrigan were the "founding mothers" of the organization. (Dorothy has often been referred to as "the mother of us all."[3]) Evangeline Machlin, although not present at this meeting, was an advisor, and Carolyn Coombs functioned as secretary. These women served as VASTA's first board members with Barbara Acker, Barry Kur, and BettyAnn Leeseberg-Lange serving as officers during the first few years of VASTA, and then they moved into positions on the board as the initial group stepped down. The original members were voice and speech teachers, trainers, coaches, and consultants. VASTA Archivist, Janet Rogers, explained:

> The term "voice and speech trainer" was first coined and presented in 1986 as a way of describing what we were. I had been teaching voice and speech for a few years but didn't know of anyone else who was doing what I was doing. Suddenly, that summer in NYC, I found myself with an identity ("Voice and Speech Trainer") and a community of like-minded colleagues. (February 2012)

At VASTA's 10th anniversary, there were 17 people who were acknowledged for their early presence and contributions when the hat (or waste basket) was passed.

Growth of the Organization

Within a year, VASTA had been formally established and held its first annual conference. VASTA was incorporated at the August conference at Pace University in New York City in 1987. Five years after its inception, VASTA had 150 members. By 1998, there were 270 members; in 2012, there were almost 500; and today, VASTA has nearly 775 active members.

The founding members established a "Statement of Purpose," and they created "Evaluation Guidelines" for voice and speech trainers and a "Code of Ethics and Guidelines for Training."[4] From the beginning, VASTA members represented a diverse cross section of the profession. They came from different parts of the United States, worked in a range of settings (university, conservatory, private practice, and media), and utilized diverse training methodologies. Business was conducted through phone calls and letters. Early on, VASTA provided advocacy for promotion and tenure procedures for voice specialists in higher education and guidelines for faculty and administrators to use in promotion and tenure assessment. Janet Rodgers, a VASTA member since 1986, describes early VASTA days as "trail-blazing through new territory. The area of voice and speech was in its infancy in institutions of higher learning, and there were very few resources available for dialect research" (February 2012).

By 1988, VASTA had 12 committees which addressed the business of membership, grants, publications, conferences, and the compilation of bibliographies. Even in its early days, VASTA had already established strong links to related organizations such as the American Speech–Language–Hearing Association, the National Communication Association,[5] the

Voice Foundation, and the National Association of Teachers of Singing. The number of positions and committees within VASTA has increased over the years in part to address the increase in membership and also to provide support for both the increased range of services provided and the expansion of VASTA's role as an advocacy group in the areas of social justice and diversity. At the time of its 10th anniversary, there were seven board members and four officers. In its 30th year, VASTA had 21 officers and committee chairs in addition to its 11 board members.

By VASTA's 10-year anniversary, the organization had a membership directory, an annual conference, a newsletter, promotion and tenure guidelines, training guidelines, a bibliography, summer and winter workshops, scholarship funds, and a thriving membership composed of global voice professionals. The president at the time BettyAnn Leeseberg-Lange noted, "VASTA has gone from a collection of teachers to an organization in which different approaches and techniques are examined, appreciated for their merits, respected for their differences, and discussed at great length" (VASTA 1996, 2). BettyAnn also observed that VASTA members had been victims of downsizing and still struggled to develop "equitable work and salary parameters" (2).

The Role and Evolution of Conferences

Since its first conference at Pace University in New York City, VASTA has held an annual conference, and conferences remain an essential function of the organization. Conferences typically have a focus topic and provide the opportunity for members to take workshops with experts in the field. Famed voice coach Cicely Berry gave a workshop at the first conference. Later conference keynote presenters have included other well-known figures in the voice world: Catherine Fitzmaurice, Jan Gist, Susana Bloch, Arthur Lessac, David Smukler, Kristen Linklater, Patsy Rodenberg, Dudley Knight, Andrew Wade, David Crystal, Rocco Dal Vera, Judith Koltai, Jeffrey Crockett, E. Patrick Johnson, Wesley Enoch, Leith McPherson, and I Wayan Dibia, among others.

The scope of the conference has grown over the years as well. The focus topic for the second conference was "Vocal Health," and the presenters included the medical voice specialist, Bob Parks. The third conference focused on the implications for voice regarding Feldenkrais and Alexander techniques. The conference title, "Awareness Enhancement Training: Making the Vocal/Physical Connections," reflected the VASTA community's inclusionary and often holistic view of training. A session at this conference was "Things That Work," which provided an opportunity for participants to share techniques, tools, and tactics; this session has subsequently been on many conference schedules, and for several years, it was moderated by founding member Bonnie Raphael. In a generous spirit of sharing, the session symbolizes the ethos of VASTA as a whole. Several early members have also recounted the crucial role that conferences played in the pre-email and pre-social media era, facilitating the exchange of ideas. A more recent favorite conference session is "The Identity Cabaret," an opportunity for VASTA members to perform material (typically original work) that is close to the heart. It was first offered at the conference in London in 2014. This event has been a feature of every subsequent conference as an opportunity to celebrate the artistry, originality, and passion of members.

Both recent and long-time members speak of the conferences as being central to their experience of the organization—a time to reconnect with old friends, to recharge as trainers, and to learn new approaches to teaching and professional practice. Eric Armstrong describes it as "revisiting a summer camp I've gone to my whole life" (June 2012). Kate Ufema sees them as "the lifeblood of the organization. There is simply no substitute for coming together, [...] playing, sharing ideas, problems, wishes and dreams" (VASTA 2003, 6). In 2004, VASTA Day was introduced and the format of the conferences expanded to include papers and presentations by members in addition to featured conference presenters.

Since its formation, VASTA has had an active relationship with the Association for Theatre in Higher Education (ATHE). Discussion at the first VASTA conference focused on the advantages (and disadvantages) for VASTA and its affiliation with ATHE, but VASTA has maintained its ties as a "focus group" (previously "forum") of ATHE. And VASTA members have presented panels, workshops, and papers on voice and speech related topics each year at annual ATHE conferences.

Over more than 30 years, VASTA has transitioned from being an organization with membership primarily from the United States to a truly global organization, first through the inclusion of international members and presenters and later with conferences abroad and the increased presence of its membership at global workshops and conferences. Nevertheless, VASTA's interest in forging international connections has been apparent from the earliest newsletters, and an international liaison position was in place by 1988. VASTA's increasingly diverse membership now includes voice practitioners on all six continents. The first conference held outside the United States was the 1999 conference in Toronto, Canada. In 2000, VASTA hosted its first internationally themed conference in Washington, DC, "Celebrating Difference: The Performing Voice from Around the World," featuring presenters from a number of different countries and cultures. The first conference outside of North America was held in Glasgow, Scotland, in 2005, and the first international and bilingual conference took place in Mexico City, Mexico, in 2010. Since then, international conferences have taken place in London, Montreal, and Singapore. VASTA's international initiative includes the goal of holding a conference outside of the United States every five years.

Expanding Connectivity

The changes that have occurred in technology since VASTA's inception have been tremendous, most significantly the internet and the profound effect this has had on the organization's ability to provide for its membership. VASTA's website, inspired by BettyAnn Leeseberg-Lange and created by Eric Armstrong, went online in 1997. Eric observed that "our publications, website, newsletter, and resources have helped to define the voice of our profession" (June 2012, 5). Founding member Lucille Rubin observed that "the new vocal science studies shared online, both in videos and in articles, have taken the mystery out of voice production and encouraged VASTA members to be versed in vocal anatomy and physiology" (June 2012, 4). In 2011, the VASTA board undertook an initiative to rebrand the organization, which included a new logo and website designs. The initiative was led by VASTA's senior director of technology, Michael Barnes, and the former president of VASTA, Patty Raun.

VASTA's listserv, "VastaVox," began in 1995 and was created by Dudley Knight. The listserv made it possible for members of the voice, speech, and acting communities to digitally discuss their concerns and interests. While VASTA's online connectivity is now also prominent on various social media outlets like Facebook and Twitter, the "Vox" continues to be an invaluable resource, and the conversation archives are accessible and searchable.

VASTA's first newsletter came out in the Fall of 1987. Jan Gist was the first editor with BettyAnn Leeseberg-Lange later assuming the role. For the first two decades, the newsletter was published and distributed to all VASTA members in the United States and abroad several times a year. In 2005, it became available electronically and was renamed the *VASTA Voice*; it is published on the VASTA website and emailed to all members. It provides information on upcoming conferences, reports on events, a message from the president, book reviews, and magazine-like articles on voice and speech related matters. VASTA's original "Code of Ethics" and "Statement of Purpose" appear in the first issues. In 1990, the "Code of Ethics" was replaced by the recent VASTA Statement of Principles on the VASTA website. Archival issues catalogue the interest of VASTA members, not only in voice methodologies and teaching strategies but also in politics and advocacy issues.

Increasing VASTA's visibility and celebrating the expertise of its members through publications had long been a goal of many VASTA members. The first VASTA-supported research project was *The Vocal Vision*, which is a book that collected 22 essays (Hampton and Acker 1997). This text contains many essays from VASTA's early members and several from VASTA Lifetime Distinguished Members. The idea for a VASTA scholarly journal (also discussed for many years) finally came to fruition with a publication in June 2000: the volume of a serialized monograph, *Voice and Speech Review (VSR)*. Founding editor-in-chief, Rocco Dal Vera, spearheaded the project and was editor for the first three volumes.[6] (VASTA now offers a research award in his name.) VASTA published the first seven volumes, publishing every other year through 2011. VASTA still sponsors the journal, but Routledge (Taylor and Francis Group) began publishing the journal in 2014, raising its profile, prestige, and worldwide accessibility. The *VSR* now publishes three online issues yearly with a printed collection at the end of each year.

Major Initiatives through the Years

White Papers

VASTA has continued to develop policy, define standards, and advocate for the voice community through the publication of seminal documents. In addition to the foundational documents in the 1980s, VASTA has produced helpful "white paper" documents to assist members and the voice community,[7] most notably a "Mission Statement," "Guidelines for Promotion and Tenure," and "Guidelines for the Preparation of Voice and Speech Teachers." VASTA also developed a "Hiring, Retention, Promotion, and Tenure Packet" for its members. In addition, many of the original guidelines and policy documents have been updated and revised. The Diversity Initiative includes the "Diversity Bibliography a Best Practices Letter to Deans and Chairs and a Diversity Statement."[8]

Named Awards

VASTA established an Honorary Membership Award in 1988, which it now calls the Lifetime Distinguished Membership Award. (Its first recipient was Evangeline Machlin.[9]) In 1993, VASTA created leadership and service awards. That same year, VASTA offered its first scholarship in memory of Clyde Vinson, a long-time VASTA member. In 2003, VASTA established a scholarship to award a young actor competing as an Irene Ryan Award finalist at the Kennedy Center American College Theatre Festival in Washington, DC. The VASTA endowment was set up in 2002 when VASTA invested $25,000.00 for the future of the organization. By 2009, the endowment had reached the $100,000.00 mark, and in honor of Kate Ufema, who had tirelessly managed the endowment, it was named the Cathryn F. Ufema Endowment. In 2008, VASTA began offering membership enrichment grants that provide partial support for regional workshops. The Dorothy Mennen Research/Development Grant was also offered for the first time in 2008. Three more recent awards encourage scholarship in the area of voice and speech: the Dudley Knight Award for Outstanding Vocal Scholarship, the Rocco Dal Vera Graduate Research Award, and the VSR Forum Article of the Year Award.

By the beginning of the twenty-first century, the increased complexity of VASTA's structure (and finances) was apparent. Membership categories changed, and for the first time, organizational membership was included. In 2002, VASTA received grants to support the publication of the journal. In 2002, former president Kate Ufema described VASTA as a "hard working, creative, innovative, solvent organization with one goal and one goal only: to serve its members and the advocacy of our profession" (VASTA 2002, 4). Kate noted a shift in the way that academia and other theatre practitioners "recognize, respect and seek out our expertise" (5).

Diversity

In late 2004, the board held a goal-setting retreat attended by 24 current and past board members to set VASTA's goals for the next 10 years. The main themes were diversity, pedagogy, and internationalization. The vision statement that resulted was published on VASTA's website.[10] The makeup of VASTA at that point was 85% academic voice trainers and 15% private practitioners. VASTA members worked in professional theatre, film, clinical settings, and the corporate world. This committee noted how many of its members were middle-aged and emphasized the need to attract a younger and more diverse group of people to VASTA.

In response, VASTA established a diversity committee in 2005 to explore issues of diversity within the organization; they sought diversity not only in ethnicity and in language but also in physical ability, professional outlook, and pedagogy. A diversity document was presented and discussed at the 2006 conference. In 2009, growing out of the diversity initiative, VASTA published "Academic Theater Profession: A Guide to Best Practices".[11] In 2010, a diversity, teaching, and learning survey was distributed to members in an effort to gain information to help guide the diversity initiative. As an outgrowth of this effort, the 30th anniversary conference was held in Chicago with sessions on the politics of race and identity in performance with an emphasis on the implications for voice and speech training.

Connections

VASTA has continued to foster its connections to other organizations in related fields and in 2005 worked with the National Association of Teachers of Singing (NATS) and the American Speech-Language-Hearing Association (ASHA) to produce a joint statement on "The Role of the Speech Language Pathologist, the Teacher of Singing and the Speaking Voice Trainer in

Voice Habilitation" (ASHA 2005). VASTA has also become an honorary member of the following organizations: New York Eye and Ear Infirmary, Actors' Equity Association, and NATS. Moreover, the 2018 VASTA conference in Seattle will be a joint conference with the Pan-American Vocology Association (PAVA). The conference theme will be "Soma and Science: Bridging the Gap in Interdisciplinary Voice Training."

Additional Aims

VASTA has continued to develop new initiatives in order to better serve its membership and the voice community at large. The 2016 compensation and credit survey gathered useful data to help VASTA members position themselves in the market place. The VASTA Fellows Program was instituted in 2006 with the aim of connecting VASTA representatives with institutions in need of workshops, master classes, and symposia. In 2009, the Teaching and Learning Committee was formed to foster conversation and enhance attentiveness to the craft of teaching. VASTA continues to expand its international character as an organization, and, in keeping with this philosophy, VASTA recently replaced the International Committee with the Global Membership Group. New scholarships reflect VASTA's commitment to community engagement, diversity, and international outreach. For example, the conference Grant for Interdisciplinary Engagement enables VASTA members to participate in conferences outside of the area of voice and speech training. The International Scholarship gives VASTA the benefit of hearing the voices and ideas of international practitioners and offers conference scholarships to members from outside of the United States and Canada. Conference scholarships are also offered to high school and middle school teachers.[12]

Continued Vision

In 2013, VASTA held a "Vision Retreat," the third planning session in VASTA's history, to determine the course of the organization for the next 10 years. The resulting visioning statement acknowledged VASTA's long-standing commitment to advancing the field, the professional development of its members, publishing, mentorship, diversity, advocacy, and international growth. While maintaining these on-going initiatives, the board announced plans to use the following three charges to guide the organization as it moved into the future:

- *Share* within our VASTA circle by increasing opportunities to learn from each other's expertise, hear one another's stories, open conversations, provide mentorship, and nurture leaders.
- *Expand* outside our VASTA circle by creating initiatives to learn from other fields, invite new members in, and bring students to conferences.
- *Engage* with individuals and groups outside our field, offering our work to help empower their voices while opening ourselves to what we may learn in the exchange. (VASTA 2013, 1)

The charge to "provide mentorship and nurture leaders" has led to the Early Career Leadership Initiative, a move designed to benefit early career members; they attend a year of board meetings and learn the inner workings of the organization.

Part of VASTA's mission is to advance the visibility of the voice in the world, and social media has also become an increasingly important part of this. VASTA's Voices and VASTA International collaborations also offer a forum for information gathering and international collaboration. The #MyVoiceCan blog, established in 2017, provides an opportunity to feature the work of different artists and keeps the membership informed about how voices are being used to impact different communities around the globe.[13]

Conclusion

From its inception, VASTA has responded to and been instrumental in significant changes in the field of voice and speech. In 1988, Dorothy Mennen decried the lack of respect for what we do; she noted that in an announcement offering the first "comprehensive, advanced training program in voice" that there was no voice teacher or trainer named (VASTA 1988, 7). She offered the parallel of a major hospital opening a surgical unit while listing everyone involved except the surgeon. Twenty-five years later, Bonnie Raphael remarked on "the development of strong graduate training and several degrees in the field of voice and speech (June 2012). She also noted that "more interaction (rather than competition) between singing teachers, speech teachers, speech pathologists, voice specialists, dialect specialists, voice scientists, and others is now the rule rather than the exception" (June 2012). She credits this development with the technology and workshops currently available for producing more knowledgeable, more skilled, and more collaborative coaches and teachers. Carol Pendergrast credits VASTA with providing "inspiration, information, networking and respect for our profession" (June 2012).

Continually, members credit VASTA with nurturing friendships and collegial relationships, increasing skills, and creating respect for the voice and speech profession. The achievements of VASTA (a relatively small organization staffed exclusively by volunteers) over the past several decades have been nothing short of remarkable. VASTA moves forward with a strong organizational structure, enterprising leadership, and members who are passionately committed to its success.

Notes

1. This article used the collective information in the VASTA newsletters and interviews from members to create the narrative of this historiography. All quotes from personal communication are cited with months and dates. The archived newsletters can be found at www.vasta.org. This paper was first presented at the 25th anniversary VASTA conference. The article has since been updated to reflect changes in the organization.
2. VASTA Archivist, Janet Rogers, notes that the National Educational Theatre Conference was a transitionary conference in 1986. The American Theatre Association (ATA) dissolved in 1985, and the Association for Theatre in Higher Education (ATHE) began in 1986 shortly thereafter. VASTA has and continues to have a close relationship with ATHE; nevertheless, the original founders of VASTA wanted a unique organization.
3. Upon Dorothy Mennen's passing in 2011, VASTA created the Dorothy Mennen Research/Development Grant in her honor. For more information, see https://www.vasta.org/mennen-scholarship.
4. All of which can be found on VASTA's website www.vasta.org in the newsletter archives.
5. From 1970 to 1996, it was known as the Speech Communication Association.

6. For details about the geniuses of the *Voice and Speech Review*, see Dal Vera's editorial in the inaugural volume (Dal Vera, Rocco 2000).
7. White paper documents are authoritative guides created by governmental agencies and academic organizations meant to problem solve specific issues.
8. All of the discussed documents can be found at https://www.vasta.org/overview.
9. For a complete list of Lifetime Distinguished Members, see https://www.vasta.org/distin guished-members .
10. To read the complete vision statement, see https://www.vasta.org/m-p-statements.
11. For the full statement, see https://www.vasta.org/vasta-best-practices-letter-to-deans-and-chairs-diversity .
12. For details on VASTA awards, grants, and scholarships, please see the resource section of www.vasta.org.
13. See https://www.vasta.org/overview for more information.

Disclosure statement

No potential conflict of interest was reported by the author.

References

ASHA. 2005. "The Role of the Speech-Language Pathologist, the Teacher of Singing, and the Speaking Voice Trainer in Voice Habilitation." Technical report. Accessed May 1, 2018. https://www.asha.org/policy/tr2005-00147.htm

Dal Vera, Rocco. 2000. "Letter from the Editor." *Voice and Speech Review* 1 (1): 4.

Hampton, Marion, and Barbara Acker. 1997. *The Vocal Vision: Views on Voice by 24 Leading Teachers, Coaches and Directors*. New York: Applause Books.

Sansom, Rockford. 2018. "A Guide to Publishing in the *Voice and Speech Review*." *Voice and Speech Review* 12 (1): 1–10. doi:10.1080/23268263.2018.1436750.

VASTA. 1987. "Fall Newsletter." https://www.vasta.org/newsletter-past/index.html

VASTA. 1988. "Spring Newsletter." https://www.vasta.org/newsletter-past/index.html

VASTA. 1996. "Fall Newsletter." https://www.vasta.org/newsletter-past/index.html

VASTA. 2002. "Spring Newsletter." https://www.vasta.org/newsletter-past/index.html

VASTA. 2003. "Fall Newsletter." https://www.vasta.org/newsletter-past/index.html

VASTA. 2013. "VASTA Mission Statement." Accessed May 1, 2018. https://www.vasta.org/m-p-statements

The Rationale and History of Vocology

Ingo R. Titze

ABSTRACT

The definition of vocology is re-stated and its existence as a discipline for the study of all forms of vocalization across species is rationalized. A brief historical sketch is given regarding the birth of vocology and its progression in the last three decades. An explanation is offered why vocology parallels audiology to some extent and why vocologists and audiologists would benefit from more interaction.

Definition, Rationale, and Scope of Vocology

In its broadest definition, vocology is the study of vocalization. Vocology includes the exploration of the full capability of human and animal sound production, much of which is part of human speech. Vocology also includes the mechanical and electronic simulation of vocalization. For professional practice, a secondary definition of vocology is the science and practice of voice habilitation. This definition has been in existence for nearly three decades (Titze 1990), but much has been clarified and formalized since then. It is worthwhile to quote directly from the textbook by Titze and Verdolini-Abbott (2012):

> In its broadest sense, vocology is the study of vocalization. This can include every aspect of human and animal sound-making in airways within the body. As a professional discipline, we give a narrower focus within this book: the science and practice of voice habilitation, which includes evaluation, diagnosis, and behavioral intervention. The emphasis in this definition is on habilitation rather than rehabilitation. Restating from Principles of Voice Production (Titze 1994, 2000), "Habilitation is the process of *enabling*, *equipping for*, or *capacitating*. Voice habilitation is therefore more than repairing a voice or bringing it back to a normal state. It is the process of building and strengthening the voice to meet specific needs." For the majority of people, normal (unassisted) vocal development in any society is sufficient to meet both occupational and recreational needs. Although "sufficient" may be difficult to define in precise terms, one could claim that it involves a perceptual quality that lies within social norms, is expressive when necessary, and is able to produce intelligible speech at a distance of a few meters. Special voice needs may be associated with occupation, recreation, or expression of specific personality traits and emotions. These normal and special needs become the target for vocologists in terms of prevention of disorders, evaluation, and intervention. (11–12)

Mammals, birds, and reptiles vocalize to communicate one or more of the following: warn others of danger, express hunger, pain, or other discomforts, locate or be located, express emotion (aggression, fear, love, joy), demonstrate artistry, convey messages, be identified by others (or not), attract a partner, show strength and fitness, or express gender and age. The systematic study of the production, reception, and perception of sound for all these communicative purposes is the full scope of vocology. Interesting books for those who wish to become eclectic vocologists are Marler and Slabbekoorn (2004) and Bradbury and Vehrencamp (2011).

The following focus areas have been formally adopted for study by the Pan-American Vocology Association (PAVA), Resolution 1017 C:

(1) Singing (solo and choral)
(2) Efficient voice use in speaking
(3) Vocalization for acting and professional speaking
(4) Vocalization for meditation
(5) High-energy calling (military, sports, construction sites, emergency)
(6) Animal vocalization
(7) Human primal vocalization
(8) Vocalization for general health and improved body function
(9) Machine vocalization (voice simulation)
(10) Amplification effects on vocalization

Not all of the above vocalizations are habilitated naturally in a social context (i.e. without professional intervention). Such intervention includes voice training for special skills. Singing, chanting, calling, healthy screaming, ventriloquism, auctioneering, impersonation, vocal disguise, or imitation of animal calls, are all in the purview of professional habilitation. Vocology also includes the investigation of multiple sound sources in contemporary artistic vocalization, as well as differences between electronically amplified and unamplified voice production. Vocalization for emergency dispatching, cadence calling in athletics, and military combat are also part of voice habilitation.

A central focus of vocology is vocal fitness, which may be closely coupled to general well-being. Conversational speech alone may not guarantee a high level of vocal fitness because it seldom uses full fundamental frequency and intensity ranges, nor does it necessarily explore the wide range of vocal timbres that are possible. Developing the best vocal exercise for general health is part of habilitative vocology. Evidence is growing that heartbeat, hormone balance, respiration, emotional and social well-being, as well as some brain functions, can all be improved with singing, chanting, acting, or other exceptional vocal skills beyond conversational speech.

Recovery from vocal injury or disease involves professional intervention beyond vocology. However, evolutionary biologists believe that multiple alternative solutions for voice repair can be gleaned by studying nature's adaptations. The process relies on what evolution has offered across species based on vocal needs in light of body size, environment, and various selective pressures on oral communication. Surgical repair and voice therapy, as well as medical and dietary treatments, may all benefit from the study of nature's many alternative solutions for effective vocalization.

About one-fifth of the working population in developed countries rely heavily on their vocal instrument to carry out their professional activities. Thus, to understand vocology, one must understand what is meant by the term *professional vocalist*. We define a professional vocalist as any person who (1) relies on his or her voice as a primary tool of trade and (2) would probably seek alternate employment if the voice were to become seriously impaired. Often one thinks of professional vocalists as singers and actors. However, these performing artists are but a small percentage of professional vocalists. Teachers, telephone workers, receptionists, counselors, dispatchers, trial lawyers, and broadcasters, to name a few, form a much larger and economically significant group. For the vocologist who services such clientele, the boundaries between providing vocal training and vocal rehabilitation are often unclear. The problem is similar in sports and athletics. At what point does a physical therapist become an athletic trainer if his or her clientele is made up primarily of athletes? Vocologists are developing a set of tools that are not only useful to traditional speech-language pathologists for rehabilitation, but also to teachers of singing and other professional voice trainers.

The History of Vocology

The first written appearance of the word vocology was the title of a brief column written for the National Association of Teachers of Singing Journal by this author (Titze 1990). It was a plea for a united effort among voice professionals to make voice habilitation a discipline. A rationale for a curriculum in vocology was presented soon thereafter (Titze 1992). The first journal to carry vocology in its title was *Logopedics Phoniatrics Vocology* (Titze 1996), formerly the *Scandinavian Journal of Logopedics and Phoniatrics*. The name change occurred with Vol. 22 in 1997. The following year, Verdolini (1998) authored a booklet entitled a *Guide to Vocology*, published by the National Center for Voice and Speech. At the same time, Verdolini and Titze established a vocology specialty track in speech-language pathology at the University of Iowa. This track included didactic coursework in Voice for the Actor, taught by faculty in the Theatre Department, as well as Vocal Pedagogy for Singers, taught by faculty in the School of Music. The remaining courses were offered by faculty in the Communication Sciences and Disorders Department. They included Principles of Voice Production and Instrumentation for Voice Analysis.

The Summer Vocology Institute began in the year 2000 at the Denver Center for the Performing Arts as an integral teaching mission of the National Center for Voice and Speech (NCVS). In 2009, the NCVS moved its headquarters to the University of Utah, where the Summer Vocology Institute has been administered to this day. The Pan-American Vocology Association was established as a legal 501c(6) entity in 2014. It is a membership-driven organization with elected officers. The current President is Leda Scearce. One of PAVA's recent resolutions has been to accept and promote training grounds for vocology in various degree-based and certificate-based programs all across the United States and other countries. Various forms of vocology training are now offered at New York University, Shenandoah University, University of Texas at San Antonio, University of Kansas, Westminster Choir College, to name a few. Non-university-affiliated private entities are also training vocologists (e.g. Vocology in Practice). PAVA is in the developmental phase of administering a "PAVA Recognized Vocologist" credential that will test the knowledge base and experience in this field.

Formalizing vocology as a discipline reverses history somewhat. Less than a century ago, departments of speech pathology and audiology tended to grow out of departments of communication studies, which included rhetoric, oration, theatre arts, and broadcast journalism in many instances. Thus, the training of public speaking was once combined with the science of human sound production, transmission, and reception. When communication sciences and disorders began to expand, there appeared to be a need to separate normal speech, hearing and language (and the related disorders) from the *art* of speaking. For vocologists the need is reversed, at least partially. Advancing knowledge in voice science while at the same time supplementing such knowledge with selected traditions in the arts and humanities of voice production seems profitable.

A Potential Partnership Between Vocology and Audiology

To some degree, vocology parallels audiology, which is broadly defined as the science of hearing. In professional terms, however, it is primarily the science and practice of aural *re*-habilitation. A much larger percentage of the human population relies on normal aural skills as opposed to exceptional aural skills, but the percentage that requires extraordinary hearing training is not known to this author. Musicians and audio forensic experts are in the category, as perhaps are animal behavior biologists.

Scientifically, vocology parallels audiology because in both cases, there is a primary organ in the human body that becomes the focal point. In vocology it is the larynx, the main instrument for sound production, and in audiology it is the ear, the main instrument for sound reception. Both of these organs are dependent on the nervous system to transduce and organize the signals for the purpose of meaningful communication. The medical profession has given specialty labels to the treatment of these two sound transduction organs, namely laryngology and otology.

The most likely persons who coined the word audiology were Hallowell Davis and Raymond Carhart in the 1940s (as cited in Wikipedia). Audiology was previously known as *Auricular Training,* suggesting an habilitative component. The first university course in audiology in the United States was at Northwestern University in 1946, taught by Raymond Carhart. The discipline grew in response to hearing loss among World War II veterans.

When I took my first courses in communication sciences and disorders in the late 1960s, sound production and sound reception (and perception) by humans were always taught in the same series of lectures. It was rare that range of frequency and acoustic power produced by the larynx were not immediately related to range of frequency and power received by the auditory system. I studied the classic books of Fletcher (1953) and Flanagan (1965), both of which drew strong parallelism between voicing and hearing.

Consider first the anatomic and physiologic similarities. Neural signals activate the posturing muscles of the larynx to set up a glottal configuration. Airflow is produced to vibrate the vocal folds. This tissue vibration is converted to acoustic waves in the *larynx canal* (the epilarynx tube). These acoustic waves further propagate through the vocal tract and radiate from the mouth. On the reception side, the radiated sound is received by the outer ear (the equivalent of the vocal tract), elevated in pressure by the *ear canal* (the equivalent of the larynx canal, or epilarynx tube), and applied to the eardrum (the equivalent of the vocal folds). Cochlear fluid mechanics, the equivalent of glottal airflow mechanics in vocalization, excites the hair cells to transmit electrical signals to the brain via the auditory nerve. The receptor neurophysiology parallels the motor neurophysiology in the laryngeal muscles.

Over the years, the partnership between voice science and hearing science has been diminished. Vocalization is aligned more with speech and language. In Europe, this alliance is demonstrated by the title of the journal *Logopedics, Phoniatrics, and Vocology.* Interestingly, however, the older alliance still exists in Europe. For example, some academic departments in France use the term *Audio-phonologie* to describe their disciplinary alliance.

We might pose the question: What is more important for a voice trainer or a singing teacher, to have a good ear or to have a good larynx? A large debate could ensue on this issue. Certainly, the terminology we use to describe voice production in the studio is more related to hearing science than voice science. We tell students to change pitch, loudness, timbre (or voice quality), roughness, and ring. All of these are perceptual terms. Even tremor, vibrato, and register are perceptual terms that need to be cast into production terminology like amplitude modulation, frequency modulation, or spectral tilt. We talk about loudness, but never use sones to quantify it; we talk about roughness, but rarely frame it in terms of critical band theory; we talk about pitch, but rarely recognize that it depends on timbre; we talk about vocal fry, but don't relate it to periodicity detection in the auditory system. These examples demonstrate that sound reception and sound production belong together.

Summary

Vocology had its birth about 30 years ago and has enjoyed a steady growth period. Standards and credentials are being developed by the Pan-American Vocology Association. Educational departments in colleges and universities are realizing that old compartmentalizations for the study of voice are giving way to more contemporary approaches with scientific underpinnings.

Disclosure Statement

No potential conflict of interest was reported by the author.

References

Bradbury, J. W., and S. L. Vehrencamp. 2011. *Principles of Animal Communication.* 2nd ed. Sunderland, MA: Sinauer Associates.
Flanagan, J. L. 1965. *Speech Analysis, Synthesis, and Perception.* Berlin: Springer Verlag.
Fletcher, H. 1953. *Speech and Hearing in Communication.* Princeton, NJ: Van Nostrand.
Marler, P., and H. Slabbekoorn. 2004. *Nature's Music: The Science of Birdsong.* San Diego, CA: Elsevier.
Titze, I. R. 1990. "Vocology." *National Association of Teachers of Singing Journal* 46 (3): 21–22.

Titze, I. R. 1992. "Rationale and Structure of a Curriculum in Vocology." *Journal of Voice* 6 (1): 1–9.

Titze, I. R. 1994. *Principles of Voice Production*. New York: Prentice-Hall.

Titze, I. R. 1996. "What is Vocology?" *Scandinavian Journal of Logopedics and Phoniatrics* 153.

Titze, I. R. 2000. *Principles of Voice Production*. Salt Lake City, UT: National Center for Voice and Speech.

Titze, I. R., and K. Verdolini-Abbott. 2012. *Vocology: The Science and Practice of Voice Habilitation*. Salt Lake City, UT: National Center for Voice and Speech.

Verdolini, K. 1998. *Guide to Vocology*. Salt Lake City, UT: National Center for Voice and Speech.

Index

For Product Safety Concerns and Information please contact our EU
representative GPSR@taylorandfrancis.com
Taylor & Francis Verlag GmbH, Kaufingerstraße 24, 80331 München, Germany